1

The Great Locked Ladies Room Caper

Author's Note: I feel that it might enhance your enjoyment of the following reading if you knew that this entire novella was written while the author had a very full bladder, so while she was writing about all of the bursting and desperation and peeing and bladder torture in the novel she was also living it every moment that she was writing it. Enjoy!

1

The music blazed loudly to the point where Jill was starting to feel that her ears were hurting. But she looked at her watch and knew that the intermission was coming soon enough. That's what they were all really looking forward to. Jill was actually not very big on concerts but her two friends James and Jack were convinced that this would be a great place for sightings of women desperate to go to the bathroom, a fetish that the three of them all shared.

Jill had always felt like she was an odd person, not just because she had recently realized that she was a lesbian, which was actually almost mainstream now. The thing that she found made her feel isolated was the fact that her primary turn on was seeing other women in the throes of desperation for a bathroom. Just watching women squirm, cross their legs and go out of their minds for need of a toilet was the most exciting thing in the world to her. She always wanted to find other women who were into the similar and obscure fetish of bladder desperation, or omorashi as it was known in Japan, but what she found ended up being Jack and James, two guys at her college who by an extreme coincidence shared the same fetish that she did – seeing women going out of their minds desperately in need of a toilet!

It all happened kind of by accident, or foolishness on Jill's part. One day at college while taking notes in class Jill had handed Jack her Internet device so that he could copy her notes. She was mortified when she realized that she had accidentally kept one of the tabs on her device open to a website about female bladder desperation.

"What's this?" Jack said as he looked at the device with a smirk. "Female bladder desperation, the Internet's top omorashi website."

Jill felt like she could absolutely die. Here was this guy in her class that she saw every day that has to borrow her device for a minute so he could copy some notes that she had taken, and she foolishly had forgotten to close the tab to the Internet porn site that she was looking at!

"That's nothing," Jill said as she took back the device and quickly closed the tab. "It's probably just an advertisement or something like that." But her blushing and her nervousness over the whole thing gave her away. She never had the greatest poker face.

"Hey no judgment," Jack said as he watched Jill frantically close up the website. "We are all into different things."

"I swear that it was just an advertisement, I don't even know what it was, it sounds like something Japanese."

"Calm down, like I said I don't judge or anything like that. But thank you for letting me look at your notes and everything, you really saved my ass this time. You always get such good grades so I know that you must take good notes."

"You're just lucky that it was on an Internet device, if you saw my handwriting you would never be able to read my notes. I can't even read my notes to myself!"

The two of them laughed awkwardly but by then class was over and Jill thought and hoped that that would be the last that it was ever spoken of. She couldn't believe how careless she had been to have kept a tab like that opened on a device that she used to take notes at school, but she felt like checking the website during the day and she must just have forgotten to close it.

"Stupid Jill," she said as she smacked herself in the forehead. "Do you want everyone in school to know that you're some type of weird pervert? But speaking of desperation – "Jill started to make her way towards the ladies room. As usual there was a line, there was always a line. Not that she would mind under normal circumstances, she liked seeing the other women in line wiggling around, in fact it was sometimes hard for her to maintain her composure while in line for the restroom, but when you only had a limited amount of time between classes to use the bathroom you had to prioritize.

"Hurry up I really have to go!" Jill said as she danced around in the line. She noticed that the woman in front of her was also tapping her foot nervously and Jill couldn't help but get excited. As the woman entered the toilet stall and made a loud hissing pee Jill began to feel somewhat weak at the knees.

Finally the woman came out and Jill ran into the bathroom, jerked her panties down and gained sweet relief. That class was 2 1/2 hours and by the end of class she always really needed to go to the bathroom. Jill would have liked to take her time and make some of the other woman waiting miss out on the chance to go to the bathroom, but she knew that she had to get to class and she didn't want to be late, so she flushed the toilet and was on her way.

Later that afternoon when all her classes were done Jill was walking back to the dorms when she saw Jack running towards her with another guy that she vaguely remembered was named James.

"Hey Jill!" Jack said as he waved as he and James walked over.

"Hi Jack," Jill said. "And you're James right?"

The two of them nodded.

"What can I do for you?" Jill asked.

"Jill I don't want to sound weird or creepy or anything," Jack said as he looked at James before looking back at Jill.

"Which is exactly what someone says before they say something weird or creepy," Jill said raising her eyebrow.

"Your website is totally hot!" James blurted out.

"My what?" Jill said playing ignorant.

"Shut up dude," Jack said. "Jill I hope that this doesn't sound weird, but I know that that website on your tablet was not just an advertisement. That website that you were on, well I am a member and I recognized your username."

"I totally love your website!" James said. "You write some of the hottest female desperation stories that I have ever read."

"I think you probably have me confused with someone else," Jill said as she tried to walk away.

"Dude, shut up," Jack said as he covered up James's mouth. "You have to forgive James as he's a bit rude and overenthusiastic. I would just like to say that I know your identity on that website. I have actually suspected it for a while because I knew it was someone at our school, but who knew that every day I was sitting next to the girl who has one of the best desperation blogs on the entire Internet, I feel like I am meeting a celebrity. You describe the experience of being desperate so well that you obviously must be an experienced expert."

"Really," Jill said before covering up her mouth. Why did she always let flattery give her away like that?

"Ha, it is your website, I knew it!" James said as he clapped his hands together. "Do you think I can have your autograph?"

"Oh my God this is the most awkward experience of my life," Jill said now clearly blushing and wanting to get away from the situation.

"You shouldn't be embarrassed," Jack said. "I know you probably feel really weird about this right now, but I mean what I said, you are like a celebrity in the desperation community."

"Please don't tell anyone!" Jill shouted, not realizing she had totally given herself away. "If anyone at school found out I would be mortified."

"I swear on my life I would never tell anyone," Jack said. "I know what it's like to have a fetish that most people seem to think is rather weird and I know how awkward it can be to have a fetish that might not be widely approved of. That is why I would never out somebody about their sexuality or their personal sexual interests. I'm not a jerk, or a creep, I totally swear. It's just, well isn't it amazing when you find someone who shares your interest?"

"I guess so," Jill said still feeling extremely awkward.

"In your blog you kind of complain about how you don't have enough sightings and experiences," James said. "But I mean the few that you have had, the way you describe them, they are just amazing!"

"How would you like to go to a place where you could see a ton of female desperation?" Jack asked.

Jill had to admit that she was suddenly intrigued. "You know a place where there is great female desperation?"

"There is this place we go to that frequently holds concerts and the lines to the bathrooms are extraordinary!" James shouted. "We are talking lines like dozens of men and women deep, all squirming and going crazy, but mostly women, because guys will just pee anywhere."

Jack and James laughed and slapped each other five.

"Well three cheers for male urinary privilege," Jill said with a roll of her eyes.

"So we were kind of wondering if maybe you would like to come to the concert with us this weekend." Jack asked.

"You mean like a date?" Jill asked. "You do remember that I am a lesbian right?"

"We totally respect that," James said. "Don't think of it as a date, think of it as three friends enjoying a shared interest."

"I'm not really big on going to concerts," Jill said.

"That's exactly why you don't have more good sightings and experiences!" James said. "If you got out a little bit more you would see all sorts of interesting things and people, people like women desperately in need of a toilet."

Jill shook her head. "Seems weird to go to a concert just to watch women squirming around in line for the toilet, I mean as much as I enjoy seeing that I usually don't go out specifically looking for it."

"Well we have an extra ticket and we would hardly want it to go to waste," Jack said. "If you don't want it I don't know anyone else who does. I hope you don't think that we're weird or anything like that. It's just so great to discover someone that shares the fetish and can share it from a female perspective like that. It would certainly give you something to write about in your blog!" James took out a ticket and handed it to Jill. "Well think about it, we were going to catch a bus in the afternoon. The concert is not very far away. If you want to go let us know and we will tell you where to meet so that we can catch the bus." Jack handed Jill his email address which she put in her pocket.

"I'll think about it," Jill said as she took the ticket and the address.

Jill really debated about it until late in the evening. She felt weird going to a concert with two guys that she didn't know all that well except as classmates, but they seemed like nice enough people. To her it felt a lot like a date, but at the same time maybe they just had a point, maybe it was just three people sharing a common interest. She would have preferred to find another woman who shared the fetish, but finding two guys who were into it, it made her feel somewhat less alone. After much debating she decided that she would go to the concert. She figured it would be in a highly visible public place so she figured it was probably safe, and she knew Jack a long time and knew him to be a good person, even though she didn't know James as well. In the end she decided to email them and confirm that she would go, it would be interesting.

2

"How do you like the concert?" Jack asked Jill.

"What, I can barely hear you over the sound of this noise?!" Jill shouted. She could actually feel the ground vibrating from the loudness of the music, which didn't help given the fact that she could also feel the vibrations in her bladder, which was beginning to get rather full.

"It's almost intermission," James said with a smirk. "Just when they are going to have a surge for the bathrooms!"

That was when Jill realized something terrible that she couldn't believe she hadn't even considered. The fact was that she had to pee pretty badly but she felt really self-conscious at the idea of the guys seeing her desperate in line like that. She had come here anticipating that they would get to watch *other* women desperate, she hadn't even considered the fact that they would see her obviously desperate as well, and knowing that they shared the fetish made her feel extremely awkward about that. Even amongst people who didn't have the fetish she tended to conceal her need to go.

"So how long do the lines tend to get?" Jill asked as she tried to cross her legs as subtly as possible.

"Jill I am telling you they are totally epic," Jack said. "We have actually come to this concert like every year simply because they never provide enough restrooms. You have thousands of people here and maybe a couple of dozen porta potties. Whoever plans these things I suspect might be into desperation as well."

"If you were a woman you would realize that they never provide enough female restrooms anywhere," Jill said.

"Hi five to that!" James said as he slapped Jack a high-five right in front of Jill's face.

"We are now going to have an intermission," the announcer said.

"Bathroom surge time!" Jack said as everyone began getting up.

The three of them were somewhere in the middle of the rows of seats that were set up so they waited for large numbers of people to clear out. Jack and James began walking over to the nearby field.

"Guys aren't the porta potties that way?" Jill said pointing in the opposite direction.

"Yeah we'll be right there," Jack said as he started walking off with James.

"Where are you guys going?" Jill asked.

"We're going to pee," James said as he and Jack began walking towards the field. "You're welcome to join us if you want."

"Aren't you just going to use the porta potties though?" Jill asked.

"Hell no, the lines will be outrageous!" James said. "We'll be back in a minute."

Jill suddenly felt that she had gotten in over her head. She knew that she clearly had to go to the bathroom and now she was supposed to stand there with her best poker face as they all watched desperate ladies lineup for the porta potties while those guys were right now getting relief of their own.

"We're back," James said as he tapped Jill on the shoulder startling her.

"Don't scare me like that!" Jill shouted.

"Sorry I didn't mean to scare you," James said. "You look like you're kind of distracted."

"Sorry I was just thinking about something," Jill said as she very very subtly pressed her knees together and put her hands on them.

"Thinking about all those desperate ladies we're going to see squirming like crazy in line!" James said as he and Jack slapped each other five adding a bunch of woos as Jill slapped them five as well adding a couple of woos.

"Shall we?" James said as he pointed in the direction of the porta potties.

"Ladies first," Jack said as he looked at Jill.

"What a gentleman," Jill said as the three of them began walking over in the direction of the porta potties. As soon as they got there they saw enormous crowds blocking the way to the porta potties. Jill had to admit that she had never seen crowds like that before. There were indeed only a couple of dozen porta potties and what looked like 50 to 100 people in front of each one.

As soon as Jill saw that she froze like a deer in the headlights. It would probably take an hour to get through those lines, possibly more, and she could feel her bladder shudder at the sight of it.

"Wow we really hit the jackpot this year!" James said as he put his arms around Jill and Jack. "I think this is the biggest lineup I have ever seen in my life. Didn't we tell you would see something pretty awesome if you came to the concert with us Jill?"

Jill smiled faintly. "You certainly don't disappoint. So what do we do now?"

"Now we enjoy the real show," Jack said as the three of them approached the line. "See any signs of desperation? Maybe you can spot them better Jill because you're a woman and you notice the signs even more subtly."

"You guys see any desperation yet," Jill said pressing her knees together as discreetly as possible. Jill started looking up and down the lines and she could see clearly a couple of women doing the telltale pee dance as well as showing other signs of desperation. "Well she is obviously desperate!" Jill said as she pointed to a blonde haired woman in jeans who looked to be standing pretty still.

"How do you figure?" Jack said. "She doesn't seem to be moving at all."

Jill pointed to the woman. "Exactly, when you are really desperate sometimes it's easy to try and stand still as much. But if you look closely at the woman you can see the telltale signs. Look at the way she keeps shifting her feet and digging into the ground with her shoes. Look at the way her arms are folded and how she keeps looking ahead with that annoyed glance at the porta potty up ahead. She is staring at it like it was an oasis in the desert and she hadn't drank anything all day long."

"Hey she's right, that's a good spotting Jill," James said. "I'm glad we brought you along, you have a much keener eye to this type of stuff. I knew it was a good idea to bring a woman along to this."

Jill thought that they must be somewhat oblivious because she was standing in almost exactly the same stance as the blonde woman that the three of them all had their eyes glued to. Within a short time she began crossing her legs and looking at her watch.

"She's becoming more obvious now," Jack said as he looked at Jill who tried to stand as still as a statue.

"It's easiest to try and stand still," Jill said. "But after a certain point if you are standing up it's kind of hard to ignore the pressure that is just building up inside of you. So you can see her more subtly twitching and showing more physical signs."

"Good observations Jill," Jack said as they continued watching the blonde woman that they had been watching for nearly 15 minutes. As Jill watched the two guys watching the woman she noticed a distinct bulge in their pants but tried not to say anything because she was starting to feel awkward. The thing that somewhat annoyed her was the fact that she could tell that they were clearly very comfortable and while they were all standing staring at that blonde woman growing increasingly agitated, they didn't even think to themselves that perhaps Jill had to pee as well!

"That woman has some nice breasts too," James said as they continued to stare at the blonde woman, who Jill noticed indeed had some pretty large knockers, although as she looked at her own chest she thought to herself –

"I think Jill has bigger ones," Jack said as he and James them laughed, as if reading her thoughts.

"Thanks," Jill said not sure whether she should take that as a compliment or as two guys objectifying her. Still she had to admit that it was nice to be noticed. Yet for all their fondness for desperation, they still didn't seem to notice that Jill was getting a bit twitchier herself.

They continued watching the blonde woman for the next several minutes as she started waving from side to side dancing in place as she continued to try and look up ahead. She was only a few spots from the front and it was obvious that she was going completely crazy.

"I can't believe it but we have been watching this woman for like a half hour waiting in line," Jack said and that was when Jill checked her watch.

"Wow it really has been a half hour already!" Jill said looking at her watch hardly able to believe as she thought that it had been over 3 1/2 hours since she herself had used the bathroom. "I bet by now the intermission is over."

"That's the great thing about concerts, we can still hear the music over here," James said. "Over here where the real show is."

Finally after 40 minutes, yes an 40 entire minutes in line, the blonde woman finally opened the door to the porta potty and slammed it shut. As that happened something suddenly came over Jill. They had been watching this woman dancing in line for about 40 minutes, watching her every little movement, and for a while it was distracting Jill from her own need to go. In fact the fact that she had to go tremendously bad made it easier for her to sympathize with the woman. But now that the woman was finally getting to go, all Jill could think about was that she was getting relief at that very minute, and that made Jill absolutely furious! She had never felt so overcome with jealousy. It felt like the two of them had both been waiting there for 40 minutes together, which they technically had, but only she was getting to go.

As the blonde woman came out of the porta potty with a huge smile on her face and walked off with a look of bliss she just happened to walk by the three of them and Jill felt like she wanted to trip the woman and make her fall over.

"Wow that was an amazing sighting!" Jack said as he looked at James and Jill. "We're glad that you managed to pick up on the signs of that woman being desperate Jill."

"Yeah, aren't you glad you came along?" James asked.

"Absolutely," Jill said as she glanced over at the porta potty that the blonde woman had come from. "So do you think we should maybe be getting back to the show now?"

The two guys looked at the line and saw that it was still dozens of people long. "This line is probably gonna be here all night," Jack said. "I bet if we look carefully you can probably spot another woman desperate that we can watch for the next 40 minutes."

"Another 40 minutes!" Jill shouted.

"What's the matter Jill, you look like you're kind of annoyed," James said as the two of them looked at her and suddenly noticed her knees knocking together as she was subtly bending, but not so subtly it seemed.

"Nothing, I'm just saying that we saw what we came here to see and now maybe we should get back to our seats since the intermission is over and everything," Jill said as she tried to stand still once again.

Jack and James looked at each other before looking back at Jill. "Oh my God," Jack said as Jill could see that suddenly the revelation had hit him.

"What is it?" James asked.

Jack looked at Jill. "You haven't gone to the bathroom the entire time we were here!"

"Hey you're right; she hasn't gone to the bathroom the entire time we were here!" James shouted. "And we've been here for like 3 1/2 hours!" James pounded his fist into his palm. "Oh snap, Jill has to pee!"

"No I don't!" Jill shouted clearly being defensive.

"Then why do you keep looking over at the porta potties with that frantic look," James said.

Jill snorted. "Well that's obvious; I want to see some girls desperate and squirming in line!" She turned and began scanning the line and pointed at a large woman near the front of the line. "Look at that big fat woman, she obviously has to go!"

"I think I see a girl squirming right now," James said as he pointed to Jill and smirked and laughed.

"You definitely have to pee right now don't you?" Jack said. "Look, you are practically jogging in place."

Jill stopped moving and began slowly clapping. "Well congratulations, you have just realized the obvious. You know for two fans of female desperation you can be pretty oblivious."

James smiled. "We were so busy watching that blonde woman dancing around that we didn't even notice that Jill is clearly bursting!"

"Well of course I'm clearly bursting!" Jill said as she stomped her foot down in annoyance. "I mean I've been here just as long as you and I haven't exactly been dehydrating myself, what did you think was going to happen?"

"Wow and you didn't say anything the entire time we were watching that woman?" Jack said.

Jill couldn't help but smile. "Well I was enjoying watching her too, at least until she finally went to the bathroom, then I was just infuriated as she got to go but I didn't! Jeez guys, what did you think was going to happen when you planned this trip?"

Jack looked at James before looking back at Jill. "We were hoping to see lots of girls get desperate in line, just like you wanted didn't you?"

Jill put her palm of her hand on her forehead and began shaking her head before looking up. "You guys really do think with your Dicks you know. Here you go on this trip to go watch female desperation, but you never even considered that when you bring an actual female along with you that she would not be able to watch without participating?!"

Jack and James looked at each other before James looked at Jill. "You know I actually hadn't thought of that, but hey it's a nice surprise!"

"Well you guys came here to see a desperate girl," Jill said while crossing her legs. "Well here you go, watch the desperate girl!" Jill started jogging in place, crossing and uncrossing her legs and bending at the knees and began waving her hands around as she stepped from side to side.

Jill continued dancing around for a minute or two before she realized that she must have looked like a freaking idiot. When she finally stopped she crossed her legs and did a little bow. Jack and James looked at each other, looked at Jill and began clapping and then the three of them burst out laughing.

"Jill you are absolutely hilarious," James said as the three of them continued laughing.

Finally the three of them stopped laughing as Jill stood there with her legs very clearly crossed.

"So what do we do now?" Jack finally asked as the two of them looked at Jill and as Jill looked over at the porta potties before looking back at them.

"Oh my freaking Lord I have to pee!" Jill said as she jogged quickly over to the front of the line for the porta potties as Jack and James trailed behind her.

3

"I feel really embarrassed to have to ask you this, and normally I never would, but do you think I can cut you in line," Jill said as she went up to the fat woman that she had pointed at to the other guys earlier.

Jack and James stood there behind Jill who was standing there with her legs tightly crossed.

The woman looked at Jill with a frown. "Weren't you just pointing at me to your friends and they were laughing?"

Jill couldn't believe that the woman recognized her. "No, I wasn't pointing and laughing at you."

The woman shook her head. "I saw you pointing and laughing at me to your friends, you think I didn't notice. Everyone laughs at me because of my weight."

"I would never laugh at someone because of their weight. I wasn't pointing and laughing at you, I was pointing and laughing at something else."

"What was it?" the woman asked.

Jill racked her brain to think of some type of explanation but all she could think of was how exceptionally bad she had to go to the bathroom.

The woman opened the door to the porta potty and looked at Jill. "You think it's funny to laugh at someone's weight, well here's me laughing at the weight in your bladder right now," the woman said as she laughed and slammed the door in Jill's face.

Jill looked at the other women in line who were looking at her with a disapproving looks and shaking their heads.

"I just really have to pee!" Jill shouted.

"Well then you can wait in line like the rest of us!" said the next woman in line as the other women behind her nodded.

"Dammit!" Jill shouted as she walked to the end of the very long line. "This line is at least a half hour or more."

"Damn Jill, what are you going to do?" James asked with an obvious smirk.

"Something you guys never do, wait!" Jill said as she crossed her arms, crossed her legs and looked at the long line stretching to the porta potties.

"It looks like Jill gets to be part of the show for us," Jack said with a snicker.

Jill smiled and stuck out her tongue. "You guys really are jerks." She had to admit that while she was feeling incredibly embarrassed and self-conscious she also had to admit that being in such a desperate situation was turning her on like crazy.

"Hey look at the big fat woman from the front of the line is out of the bathroom already and it looks like she is walking this way," James said as he pointed at the woman.

"She's coming over here?" Jill said as she looked at the woman walking in their general direction. "What is she coming over here for?"

The woman waddled over to them, looked at Jill in the line and smirked.

"Hi again," Jill said while bending at the knees and crossing her legs tightly.

"Why were you pointing at me again?" the woman asked as she looked at James.

"I was pointing you out to Jill here," James said. "I was just telling her that it looks like the woman you wanted to cut in line got out of the bathroom already. I assure you that we were not making fun of your weight in any way."

"Then why were you pointing at me earlier?" the woman asked as she crossed her arms and gave them a browbeating.

"I swear that we were not making fun of your weight," Jill said as she shifted from foot to foot feeling extremely awkward because she hated confrontational situations and the only thing worse than being in a confrontational situation is being in a confrontational situation when your bladder is about to explode.

"But why were you pointing at me and laughing?" the woman said looking extremely intimidating, partially because of her large size.

"Jill was saying look at that woman I think she has to pee really bad," James said with a laugh. "I thought it was pretty funny, but I didn't mean anything malicious by it."

The woman shook her head and raised her eyebrow. "So the fact that I had to go to the bathroom really bad you find extremely funny?"

"Well – "James began saying as he shrugged his shoulders and looked at Jill who did similar.

The woman looked at Jill doing the bathroom jitterbug and finally smiled. "You know looking at you right now, you are right, it is pretty funny!"

The woman burst out laughing as James and Jack joined in and suddenly Jill found herself to be the center of attention. She didn't want to seem like the odd man out so she started laughing as well.

"I'm Barbara," the woman said.

"I'm Jack," Jack said pointing to himself. "This is my friend James and the girl in line is Jill."

"Hey," Jill said with her legs tightly crossed as she did a little wave.

Barbara shook her head again. "Still think it's funny when someone has to go to the bathroom really bad?" She looked at Jill with a stern look when she said that.

Jill shook her head while crossing and uncrossing her legs. "I sincerely apologize for laughing at you while you were waiting in line to use the bathroom. Believe me I realize that it's no laughing matter."

The woman snorted. "Sure now you realize it, now that the shoe is on the other foot."

"Hey no hard feelings," Jill said as she extended her hand out and Barbara reluctantly shook it. "If it makes you feel any better it looks like now you can laugh at me."

Barbara smiled. "You know what I think I will." Barbara burst out laughing as did Jack and James and eventually Jill joined in, although she had to admit she could barely concentrate because the pressure in her bladder was difficult to ignore. "The lines here really are ridiculous," Barbara eventually said. "I've come here every year now for several years in a row and it seems like the bathroom situation gets worse every single year."

"We come here every year too," Jack said as he looked at James and the two of them had to struggle not to snicker since that was the whole reason they did come.

"It's my first time here," Jill said as she continued to bend at the knees and rubbed her knees with her hands. "I don't go to concerts much, mainly for reasons like this. You would think that with so many people here that they would provide more toilets."

"We always just go to the bathroom in the field," James said. "It's easier than waiting in this gargantuan line."

"That's not such a bad idea if you're a guy!" Barbara said.

"I know these guys are totally oblivious," Jill said pointing at Jack and James as she crossed and uncrossed her legs. "This line is probably going to be like a half hour long."

Barbara snorted. "Girl you'll be lucky if you get to go within the next 45 minutes to an hour, that's how long I was waiting in line."

"Well maybe if you had let me cut in line I wouldn't be in this situation right now!" Jill said with sharpness in her voice that betrayed her annoyance.

Barbara shook her head. "Why should you get to cut in line? Besides you seemed to think it was so funny that I had to wait in line, maybe now you can consider this like penance and it will teach you a lesson."

James shook his head. "Jill really can be inconsiderate about the needs of others sometimes. She really did think it was pretty hilarious seeing you wiggling around in line like that, that's why I couldn't help but laugh. But it really was rather unfunny Jill."

Jill couldn't believe how James was betraying her like that, she knew that he was enjoying every minute of it but she couldn't say anything without exposing them as kinky perverts and then they would just expose her and she didn't need this to get any more awkward.

"I guess I am learning a lesson now aren't I," Jill said as she stuck out her tongue at James. She then looked at Barbara again and reached into her pocket and took out some money. "Here let me apologize for my rudeness earlier by buying you a drink."

Barbara smiled as she took the money. "Well that's awfully nice of you Jill. Now I almost feel bad that you are stuck waiting in this huge line, although I still don't think that you should have the right to cut in line. But I am rather thirsty, so thank you Jill, I think I will go get something to drink."

As Barbara waddled off to go down to the snack bar, Jack and James looked at her as Jill did as well.

"She is rather fat," James said as the woman waddled away.

"I can't believe you guys!" Jill shouted. "You made me look like the bitch in this situation. That's why I felt guilty and gave that woman some money."

"Hey you were the one who pointed at her," Jack pointed out. "But don't feel bad, I think that what you did was really nice."

"Are you guys going to head back to the concert?" Jill asked as she continued to dance in place.

James waved his hands dismissively. "Heck no, we'd rather watch the show right here! We came here to see girls desperate and you look more desperate than any other girl here."

"I guess this is like poetic justice then," Jill said as she stuck out her tongue again. That was when she saw Barbara off in the distance waddling towards them. "Hey I think Barbara's back already."

Barbara came over carrying two large drinks and handed one to Jill.

"What's this?" Jill asked as she took the drink.

"It's a peace offering," Barbara said." I can see that you are clearly not such a bad person and you gave me enough money for two drinks so I figured I would buy you a drink."

"Thank you," Jill said as she looked at the drink before laughing. "But maybe an extra-large soda isn't the best type of gift to give a girl whose bladder is about to explode!"

The four of them all laughed as Jill took a sip. "But I am thirsty," Jill said.

"You might as well have something to drink because you're not getting out of that line anytime soon," Barbara said as James and Jack laughed.

"You know that's one of the things that sucks the most about being stuck in line," Jill said as she took a sip of her soda while bending even more at the knees. "You just can't leave the line without losing your spot. You guys are all free to move about."

That was when James and Jack looked at each other and began walking around. "Hey this is pretty fun," Jack said. "You should join us Jill. Oh wait, you are stuck in line."

Even Barbara began smiling. "It is pretty nice to be able to move around." Barbara took out a $10 bill and held it up.

"What's that?" Jill asked as she took another sip of her soda while still tightly crossing her legs.

"It's $10," Barbara said as she waved the $10 in Jill's general direction. "Would you like it?"

"Sure," Jill said as she reached for it but Barbara pulled it away and put it back in her pocket. "All you have to do is get out of line."

"What did you say?" Jill said as she once again crossed and uncrossed her legs.

"I said if you want the $10 all you have to do is get out of line," Barbara said smiling.

"But if I get out of line I will lose my place in line," Jill said as she continued crossing her legs. She turned around and looked at the woman behind her. "Do you think you can save my place in line?"

"No no no," Barbara said. "You have to get out of line and come back to the concert with me and I will give you the $10. No saving places."

"But I really really have to pee!" Jill said as she bit her upper lip, crossed her legs even tighter and bent at the knees even more.

"Do it Jill!" Jack said as James nodded in agreement.

Jill gave an anguished look. "But I can't!"

"Not even for $20," Barbara said as she took out a $20 bill and waved it out of reach of the line.

Jill shook her head. "This is a super emergency! I don't think I can hold it much longer."

Barbara shook her head. "Too bad, although I fully understand, I probably wouldn't have given up my place in line for $20 or even $50. It really did feel amazing to pee, just letting it all out. I felt like I peed and peed forever and ever, just gushing right out of me."

"Oh my God," Jill said as she began jogging in place. "I really really have to go!"

"I think that tonight is the highlight of my life," James said. "What would I have to do to get $20?"

Barbara looked at Jill and then she looked at James and Jack. "I'll give you guys each $10 if you take me to the field where you peed earlier and let me watch you go. You guys probably have to go by now don't you?"

The two guys looked at Barbara and looked at Jill and nodded.

Jill could clearly see that this woman was enjoying this just as much as they were and that taking them away from the line to go relieve themselves was just another way to punish her.

"Don't worry we will be right back," Barbara said as she started going off with the guys. "We're sure you will still be there when we get back."

Jill watched as the three of them walked off into the distance. She looked at the line ahead of her and estimated she probably still had another 20 minutes left. She knew that she had to go extremely bad because she actually turned down $20 just to be able to relieve herself without further waiting. She never thought she would be desperate enough to be driven to a situation like that.

She tried her best to just focus on holding it in and within five minutes Barbara and the two guys came back all with smiles on their faces.

"Well that was an experience!" Barbara said as she patted the two guys on the back. "These guys really know how to pee, really know how to let loose. They just kept going and going and going!"

"Shut up!" Jill said as she danced from leg to leg crossing and uncrossing them like mad.

"What are you gonna do about it?" Barbara said. "Going to get out of line and stop me? Nope, you said it yourself, when you are in line you are stuck in line. You certainly wouldn't want to lose your place."

"You're all sadistic!" Jill said as her whole body was shaking.

Barbara began smiling and laughing. "You know Jill you really are pretty hilarious. This is more entertaining than the concert, which to be honest has been going downhill for the last couple of years."

"Jill really is pretty hilarious," James said.

"You think maybe I can get a picture with the girl with extreme bladder fortitude?" Barbara asked. "I'll give you the $20 if you let me take a couple of pictures with you."

"Really?" Jill said. "There isn't any type of special catch?"

Barbara shook her head. "But I want you to smile."

"That's all?" Jill asked thinking in a rather simple request.

Barbara nodded. "But also stand up straight, none of that jiggling around."

Jill knew there was a catch but she wasn't going to let this woman intimidate her so she nodded.

Barbara gave her camera to James and then she had Jill stand up straight, put her arm around her and give her a thumbs-up with a big smile. Jill took several pictures with Barbara and it actually made her feel like she really was some type of a celebrity.

"So do I get my $20 now?" Jill asked as she resumed tapping from 1 foot to the other.

"Well Jill you have been a good sport about everything so here you go," Barbara said as she gave Jill the $20 and took back her camera from James and began holding it up.

"Why are you still holding the camera up?" Jill asked as she stopped squirming around.

Barbara smiled. "No reason, I just thought it would be nice to have some video footage to remember you by."

Jill could tell that Barbara realized how self-conscious she was. "I'd rather you not film me when I am in this state."

Barbara laughed. "You mean jiggling around and everything?"

Jill nodded.

"I guess you had better try to stand still then," Barbara said with a wicked smile.

"Can you just not film me?" Jill said as her legs began shaking.

"Are you going to get out of line to stop me?" Barbara said.

Jill began to step forward but then she stopped and crossed her legs and began blushing.

"Just like I thought," Barbara said holding up her camera phone. "You're going to be a movie star."

Jill wanted to run and grab the phone from Barbara but it was almost her turn in line. Finally she was next in line.

Barbara came over just out of reach. "Do you want me to delete the video Jill?"

Jill nodded. "I would like that very much."

"Then come and take it from me," Barbara said as she began running off just as the porta potty opened up finally. Jill realized that she had to make a decision between running after Barbara and running into the bathroom. Unfortunately it was a no-brainer as she slammed the porta potty door shut, jerked down her skirt and had a pee so loud and so intense that she could feel her whole body trembling.

When she finally stepped out of the bathroom, Barbara was nowhere in sight.

"Thanks for getting that video back from her!" Jill said as she approached Jack and James.

"Well she did give you $20," James said. "And I have to say this was probably the greatest night of my life."

"Yeah mine too," Jack said. "We came here to see female desperation and my God did we see some. I think that this night is permanently etched in my mind and will be until the day I die. How about you Jill, did you enjoy yourself?"

"I think we should be getting home now," Jill said. The three of them got on the bus and Jill said very little on the way home as there was sort of an eerie silence that prevailed. They were all rather exhausted and they weren't exactly sure what to say.

"So I'll see you in class?" Jack asked as Jill got off the bus.

"Sure," Jill said.

"Jill wait," Jack said. "I hope that whatever we did today we didn't go too far over to out of line and I just hope that you had a good time."

Jill nodded. "Thank you for the tickets, I think that it was an okay time, humiliating and mortifying perhaps, but other than that a pretty fun time."

As Jack and James went back to their dorms and Jill went to hers she slowly walked down the hallway, walked into her dormitory, went into her bedroom under the covers and began masturbating until she was raw and fell into one of the deepest sleeps of her life.

4

Jill woke up the next morning hardly able to believe what had happened the day before. She had had lots of desperate experiences before but absolutely nothing that intense. She felt extremely embarrassed by the entire situation and couldn't believe that she went through with it, but she also couldn't stop thinking about it and masturbating to thoughts of it. In fact she couldn't remember the last time she had been so horny. Something about the desperation being so public made it much more intense. But as much as she liked it she couldn't picture herself having done that intentionally if she had known what was going to happen.

"I have to check the Internet," Jill said immediately as she got up that morning, or immediately after going to the bathroom anyway. As soon as she got on YouTube she started looking for all sorts of videos relating to the concert. She felt she was in the clear but then she clicked on it. The video was simply titled "crazy bitch has to pee" and as soon as she clicked the video of her dancing around in line she felt butterflies in her stomach.

Then she looked at the video to see that it also had several hundred views already and the vast majority of people liked it. She had to admit that made her feel like she was kind of a celebrity after all, but she didn't really want to be a celebrity for this. Still it didn't give away her fetish. It could just be that she had to go to the bathroom really bad in line and nobody knew how much she was enjoying it, secretly anyway.

And although she knew that it was the cardinal rule of the Internet that you never read the comments, she couldn't help but read the comments.

"Oh my God look at that crazy bitch dancing around."

"I wanted to see her wet herself."

"She looks like she is having an epileptic fit."

"I like the fact that it didn't seem like she wanted to be recorded."

She figured that she had better stop reading there as she tried to reassure herself that no one was going to recognize her in that video. The Internet was a mostly anonymous place although you could clearly see her identity in the video nobody knew her name and her name was not linked to the video in any way. Still the thought that there was a video out they are of her dancing around desperate in line looking like an escaped mental patient did make her feel a little bit strange.

She knew what she had to do next of course. She had to get immediately to blogging all about it. But as Jill typed up her experience to put in her blog she wasn't sure if she should mention that someone took a video of her because then maybe they would link the video to her account. She thought there was a slim possibility but she had to take it into consideration. Someone could read her blog and see the video online and put two and two together and then she would be totally outed.

As she thought about editing out the part where she said someone was videotaping her she hesitated. She did want to give a full account of everything that happened, and the thought of someone discovering the video almost made her kind of excited, so she decided to just leave everything as is and hope for the best.

As she was checking her email later on she realized that she got emails from Jack and James asking if she wanted to hang out and discuss what had happened. She had to admit that she was still feeling extremely awkward about the entire event and wasn't sure if she wanted to talk about it so she said that she was busy.

However as luck would have it later on Jill was walking around campus and she ran into Jack and James.

"Hey Jill," Jack said as James waved.

"Oh hi guys, how are things?" Jill said suddenly feeling on the spot.

"Everything's pretty good Jill, we were just wondering how you are doing," James said. "You're not avoiding us are you?"

"No, of course not!"

"We were just hoping that we didn't do anything that was out of line," Jack said.

"No I had a good time, I just guess I feel a little bit weird about it. I mean I have had this fetish for a long time and I have been desperate in many situations before, but I never went to a place specifically to see desperate women only to end up desperate myself."

"That was pretty awesome," James said. "I have never seen someone dancing around like you. I wish that we had a copy of that video that Barbara took. I wonder if she uploaded it to the Internet."

"Why would she do that?" Jill said, once again feeling nervous.

"Hell it's what I would do!" James said as he laughed. "A great video of a girl dancing around desperate like that, who wouldn't want that in their collection."

"So you collect videos like that on the Internet too," Jill said with a smirk.

"I think that we all probably have a pretty large collection on each of our computers," Jack said. "I mean I regularly look on YouTube and all the other major video streaming sites for desperation clips and I know that you do as well because you always post links in your blog."

"Guilty," Jill said as she raised her hand and laughed. Once again she felt butterflies stirring in her stomach at the thought of it, but then she ultimately decided that she couldn't resist. "I have something to show you guys."

Jill took out her tablet and brought up the video of her dancing in line for the porta potty.

"No way that's awesome!" James said. "I'm going to send this to everybody."

"Wait, who is everybody?" Jill said as she took back her tablet.

"I just mean we will send it around in the desperation community," James said. "Because come on it is a pretty amazing clip."

"Yet you really could be a celebrity Jill," Jack said.

"But I don't want my video all around the Internet like that, what if someone discovers who I am?"

"I don't think the odds of that are very likely," James said. "But come on, to have a video like this and not share it, it's just plain wrong!"

Jill shrugged her shoulders pretending to be nonchalant about it even though she could feel the butterflies going crazy in her stomach. "I guess the video already is out there and I'm sure that no one will link it to me or derive the fact that I was enjoying myself."

"And if they do so what?" Jack asked.

"So what, I would be outed as a pervert!" Jill shouted.

Jack laughed. "No you wouldn't Jill. Even though this would be a nice fetish video for people who share the interest, for people who don't have a desperation fetish looking at a girl dancing in line like that probably doesn't mean anything. You know how many people post all sorts of stupid things to the Internet. Someone would probably see this video and think it's just a funny video of some girl who has to pee really bad that somebody uploaded for jokes. Just like all those pictures of women who take selfies when they are in the ladies room."

"I have to admit that I have never done that," Jill said. "I am a bit self-conscious about these things."

"You look pretty hot on the toilet I bet!" James said which made Jill blush. "Sorry, I didn't mean to sound weird or anything."

Jill smiled. "I do look pretty sexy sitting up on the toilet, but I am not going to put that online!"

"Anyway Jill the reason why I emailed you before is that James and I kind of want to show you something," Jack said.

"What is it?" Jill asked suddenly curious.

"Actually it's a place," James said. "A place that we think might be a good location to see more desperation."

"What type of place?" Jill asked.

"It's about a 45 minute ride from here," Jack said. "It's actually kind of a park. This weekend there probably won't be hardly anyone there, but next weekend there is this big festival that often attracts hundreds of people to the park where they have all sorts of drinks and everything like that. We went there last year and we saw some pretty decent lines for the ladies room."

"Maybe not as big as the ones that we saw at the concert but still pretty epic ones," James said. "The park only has one toilet block so it's really not suited to accommodating really large crowds of people."

"How many toilets does it have?" Jill asked.

Jack laughed. "I know that you always like to take a tally of how many places are available to go to the bathroom at any given place, you mention it all the time in your blogs. You'll be happy to know that the men's room has four stalls and an entire wall full of urinals, like a dozen places to pee!"

"How many does the ladies room have?" Jill asked.

"We weren't able to go inside for obvious reasons," James said with a laugh. "But I thought that maybe we could go down to the park today and check it out.

Again we probably won't see anything interesting this time, but we can show you around the park. It's a nice place to hang out if you're not doing anything today."

Jill shrugged her shoulders. "I guess I don't have anything better to do, I might as well see the park."

"It's kind of in the middle of nowhere," Jack said. "But it's nice and secluded. Lots of people will probably be in the park since it's a nice weekend but it's next weekend when they are having the big festival with plenty of drinks and everything where the lines to the ladies room will probably be quite spectacular. But I thought that maybe we could just check it out right now and maybe you could even tell us how many ladies toilets there are."

"You know I have never traveled all the way to a park just to scope out the bathrooms," Jill said with a laugh. "But sure, why not, I have nothing better to do today."

"Great, let's go catch the bus, I think it leaves shortly," Jack said.

As Jill got on the bus with the three of them she couldn't help but think of how strange it was that all the sudden now she was going to places just to check out their potential for desperation, but it was kind of nice having people who understood the fetish, even if it was from a slightly different perspective. Since they were guys they would never take into consideration that even people who are into desperation, women who are into desperation that is, still like to get to go to the bathroom sometimes. Everything within moderation was always her motto and she was rather timid when it came to taking actual risks.

They had a pleasant ride to the park where they didn't really talk all that much because they were all kind of tired from the night before still.

"Here it is, Theodore Roosevelt Park," Jack said as they got off the bus. "I wonder how many parks across the country are named after him."

"Given that he was so into preserving the environment I would imagine quite a lot," Jill said. "But this place looks pleasant enough. Where are the bathrooms?"

"I like a girl who gets right down to business like that!" James shouted.

"I also kind of have to go," Jill said laughing. "I think my bladder is still kind of exhausted from last night. You know after a really big hold for a couple of days afterwards sometimes it seems like you have to pee constantly all the time? That's why you should only do stuff like this in moderation."

"The bathrooms are this way," Jack said as he pointed off in the distance.

They walked a short distance until they came to the block where the bathrooms were.

"Here it is, sadly no lines," James said as they approached the bathroom area. "I guess let's check it out."

"I'm going to scope out the ladies room," Jill said as she opened the door to find no one else in the bathroom. As she looked around she saw that there were four stalls, which didn't seem like a lot but was probably adequate for most of the time. However if there were hundreds of people at the park all at once drinking heavily over the course of several hours it was likely that the bathroom would get a high volume of usage. She could easily see how this could lead to lines. She figured that the bathroom would be in pretty much constant use which ensures a line of desperate people. And there were some nice tables right outside the bathroom area where they could sit and watch.

Jill quickly used the bathroom and noticed that the toilets were pretty nice and clean. It looked like the park maintained the bathrooms rather well.

As Jill came out of the bathroom she saw Jack and James standing there.

"So what's the good news Jill?" Jack asked.

"Well the bathroom has four stalls, which isn't a whole lot if you are expecting hundreds of people to show up. How many does the men's room have?"

"Four stalls eight urinals!" James said. "You know I almost felt like Abraham Lincoln saying that, four stalls and seven urinals ago."

"Very funny," Jill said. "You should think about becoming a comedian. But this is a point I would like to make, the guys have like three times as many places to go to the bathroom. When you have come here in previous years for this festival I bet never once has there been a men's room line."

"Not true, there was once a short one where I had to wait nearly 5 minutes," James said.

"Wow a whole five minutes, how did you manage?!" Jill said as she rolled her eyes. "And how long was the ladies room line?"

James began walking until he was several paces away to the point where Jill could barely see him and then waved as Jack and Jill followed over to where James was.

"Okay, now this is some ridiculous ass line right here," Jill said as she stretched her arms out. "I mean don't you think this is rather ridiculous."

"I do think it would be pretty great for seeing lots of desperate women squirming," James said with a smile.

"Oh I don't doubt it," Jill said shaking her head. "But this is the thing that you guys don't seem to realize, you go to all these places looking to see female desperation and you pretty much always get a free show, I mean you never have to actually wait yourself, do you?"

"I just said how we had to wait five minutes once," James said shaking his head.

"I'm talking about a real wait, like the one yesterday at the concert. Stuff like that is all too common for women to experience on a regular basis. I mean I enjoy desperation as much as the next girl, but you also have to remember that at some point I will have to use the bathroom! Sure I had fun yesterday watching the women squirming in line, but then I had to become one of them and I totally wasn't expecting that. That's the difference between us. You guys always get a free show, but I have to worry about the practical concerns. As I go to all these places with you to watch women get desperate you also have to take into account the fact that I am a woman and that I get desperate just like all the other ones and sometimes you really really don't want to have to wait an hour when you are bursting!"

"I get what you are saying Jill, I guess since we are guys we don't really see it the same way," Jack said. "I suppose that we were only thinking about our selfish pleasure and in inviting you we didn't even realize the fact that you would have to deal with the practical realities of not getting to go to the bathroom. We are so used to it just being us guys watching some squirming ladies that it's kind of weird to be doing this with an actual woman who is also into desperation but also who has to worry about getting desperate herself. I suppose that's a conundrum for every female fan of female desperation."

Jill began clapping. "Thank you, you get my point. Sure I like seeing desperation, but within a limit. Yes I had fun last night but that was pushing things way too close. I certainly don't want to have any type of an accident or anything like that."

"Then I think this event might be easier on you Jill," Jack said. "The lines get long but they are manageable long. As long as you don't wait until you are absolutely bursting before you go to the bathroom you shouldn't find yourself in any type of situation like last night."

"That is something that every girl learns quickly," Jill said. "You never wait until the absolute last minute to go to the bathroom, especially at a crowded place where there is a huge surge towards the bathroom. That was the big mistake that I made yesterday as it sort of slipped my mind. And then watching that blonde woman desperate while not even getting in line myself was my second mistake. I guess I just got so caught up in the moment I forgot all practicality altogether. But that is something that you guys probably didn't consider. You knew that you could just pee in the field, that's not an option for me. As a woman you always have to be expecting the potential for a long wait. Intermissions can mean a 25 minute line or more for a woman where a guy would just waltz in and out without a wait."

James laughed. "I guess we are learning all about the female perspective on female desperation from an expert."

"I guess I could consider myself something of an expert on the topic," Jill said as she flipped her shoulder length brunette hair and smiled. "As you know I have a whole lifetime of experiences being caught desperate so it makes you extremely cautious. But I think that you guys are right, I think that this festival would be a pretty good opportunity to see lots of people desperate and as long as I am cautious I shouldn't get myself into any type of predicament that I wouldn't want to be in. Normally I go to the bathroom long before I reach the stage of desperation so I guess I can have my cake and eat it too."

"You can watch the other ladies squirm without having to squirm yourself," James said as he high-fived Jill.

"There was just one thing that I found to be rather strange about the bathrooms here," Jill said. "While I was in the ladies room I noticed that there was a lock on the door."

"What is so strange about that?" Jack said. "Don't the stalls normally have locks on them?"

"I don't mean the stalls," Jill said as she waved them over to the bathrooms. She went to the door of the ladies room and opened it up and pointed to the inside. "It seems that the door to the bathroom itself locks from the inside."

"I wonder if it is true for the men's room as well," Jack said as the three of them went to the men's room to look at the lock on the door to find that it was exactly the same.

"Don't you think that that is weird?" Jill said. "I mean it makes sense that you would lock the stalls while you are in there but this would allow someone to lock the entire bathroom. That just seems kind of insane doesn't it? I mean I can understand how someone might want to lock the entire bathroom if they are shy about going when other people are in the bathroom, I'm a bit shy myself sometimes, but I wouldn't lock everyone else out of the bathroom just because I was using it. I mean how selfish would it be to hog the entire bathroom when there are four stalls and I would lock everyone else out until I was done?"

"It's probably because during the off-season they lock up all the bathrooms altogether," Jack said. "It probably just makes things easier."

"Oh my freaking God that's it!" James said as he approached the two of them with fist in palm.

"What's it?" Jill asked.

"Guys don't you see the implications of this," James said. "If the bathrooms lock from the inside we could easily go into the bathroom and wait until nobody was around, lock the doors from the inside and then close the doors and then no one would be able to get in!"

Jill frowned. "Well that just seems kind of wrong. Besides if you lock the bathroom there would be no lines."

James scratched his chin. "That's a good point, but think of all the desperation there would be! Think about it you guys, imagine that next week during the festival when everyone is drinking a lot and there are hundreds of people in the park, imagine what would happen if all the bathrooms were locked!"

"I think a lot of the women would probably just end up using the men's room," Jill said. "I mean I would feel weird about it but if it was a choice between that and wetting myself I would take a chance I suppose, even though I really wouldn't like it."

"Well we would lock the men's room as well," James said. "Not that it matters since we are out here in the open where men can easily just pee on a tree, so it would probably only affect the women."

"That is unbelievably evil!" Jill said.

"What, wouldn't you think it was hilarious to see an entire park full of desperate people without a bathroom available? All these women drinking and drinking only to go over to the bathrooms and push on the door only to find it locked."

"I've been in that situation!" Jill shouted. "During the last two years of high school they closed all but one of the girls' bathrooms because they found drugs and alcohol in them so I was only able to get to go to the bathroom maybe once or twice a day and it was really a pain. I would push on the doors and they would be locked and I would just kick the doors in anger. All the guys that I knew in high school thought that it was funny because their bathrooms of course where all still kept open."

"Oh my God that is fucking hilarious!" James said as he burst out laughing. "I mean that has to be the greatest thing in the freaking world."

"Not if you are a girl who doesn't want to hold your pee all day through school!" Jill shouted back as she playfully slapped James in the arm. "Although I do think that whole situation probably played a role in me developing this fetish in the first place."

"Well at least something good came out of it," James said. "But think of how great it would be to see an entire park full of desperate people for hours on end, all those women dancing around and squirming going out of their minds looking for a bathroom."

"I have to admit that is pretty funny," Jack said. "Come on Jill, even you have to admit that the whole idea of that is rather hilarious."

Jill couldn't help but burst out laughing. "Okay I'll be the first to admit it, it really is fucking hilarious, and even I cannot deny that. It's evil, but sometimes the evilest pranks are the funniest ones. Honestly the whole idea is somewhat ingenious and I have to applaud your brilliance in thinking of such a nefarious plan. But I do just have one teensy-weensy little problem with it."

James scratched his head. "What am I forgetting?"

Jill rolled her eyes. "You don't see a problem with this?"

James shook his head once again. "No, the whole plan actually seems pretty well thought out; I don't see any possible flaws with the plan."

Jill stood there tapping her foot. "Really, you don't see a single flaw with the plan? What was I just sort of lecturing you guys about not long ago? You don't see a problem here?"

Jack and James looked at each other shrugged their shoulders and shook their heads.

"Really you guys don't see a problem here perhaps from my perspective at the idea of you guys locking the women's restroom?" Jill suddenly started dancing around and put her hands up to her breasts and started jingling them around and then did a flip of her hair before spinning around. "I'm a woman numbskulls! If you lock all of the ladies rooms up as well as the men's room, then what am I supposed to do?! You totally were oblivious to the fact that while you were planning this whole lock the ladies room scheme up that the third co-conspirator in your group is a woman, a woman with a practical need to urinate at some point over the course of the entire day!"

James laughed. "Oh wow, I guess I forgot about that."

"Of course you did, you guys never seem to think about anything other than seeing women desperate!" Jill said as she pointed to herself. "I on the other hand have to consider the practical implications of all these evil little plans we think of. Granted I will admit that it's a hilarious idea, but you can see why it wouldn't work out well for me."

"It reminds me of something that I did once," James said laughing. "Once I went around putting all of these out of order signs on all these ladies rooms when they were perfectly available. It was funny because I saw these women going up to the bathroom and looking at the sign and frowning and the looks on their faces, absolutely priceless!"

"Oh my God that is so freaking wrong!" Jill shouted shaking her head. "Although I will admit that it probably was priceless to see the looks on their faces. I am sure that the look on my face the few times I have seen an out of order sign on the toilet must have been a Kodak moment, but still you can see why I couldn't really go through with this whole plan. Not just because it seems especially malicious, even if it would be hilarious, but because practically speaking it would not end well for me."

James snapped his fingers. "Dammit Jill we can't have a great hilarious idea like this and not go through with it. Wouldn't you love to see this whole plan put into motion?"

Jill rolled her eyes. "Yes it would be funny for me to *watch all the desperation* but I don't think that my own bladder could go all day without a bathroom and I certainly do not want to have an accident."

"Can't you just go squat in the bushes?" James asked.

Jill shook her head. "No I don't know how to go to the bathroom outdoors and even if I did I wouldn't because I'm not going to expose my ass for all the world to see in the middle of a public park!"

"Wait I think I might have a solution to this," Jack said. "You guys follow me."

"Where are we going?" Jill asked. "We have been walking for a while."

"It's a bit out of the way but I think that it will provide a solution to your problem Jill," Jack said as they walked to the far end of the park out of the way and away from where all the people congregated.

"What are we doing all the way out here?" James asked.

"Remember last year?" Jack said as he walked a few paces through the bushes and that was when he saw it. "Tada!"

"What is it?" Jill said as she looked at it.

"It's a porta potty!" Jack said as he went over to it and opened it up. "See and it's fully operational."

"Why are you showing me this?" Jill asked.

"This is the perfect solution to the problem!" James said. "This porta potty is entirely out of the way and no one knows it exists. So you see if we lock all the ladies rooms that will make everyone desperate because they don't know about this hidden porta potty. So if you need to go to the bathroom during the day you will have this as sort of a plan B to make sure that you have something to fall back on."

"How do we know that it will still be open?" Jill said.

"We come to this park pretty regularly and it has been there for basically forever," Jack said. "Trust me Jill they always keep this here for some of the park workers who come during the off-season."

"I'll be honest I'm not the biggest fan of porta potties," Jill said as she looked it over. "Although to be fair as far as porta potties go this is one of the nicer looking ones I have seen."

"I told you that no one knows it exists so it stays in pretty good shape," Jack said as Jill looked inside.

"So what do you say Jill, are you ready to witness the desperate experience of a lifetime?" James asked as he and Jack looked at her with big smiles.

"I think I need time to think about this," Jill said. "I mean it's kind of risky, what if we get caught?"

"Look I don't think that we will, if we just lock the bathrooms we can always say it was an accident or something," James said. "Besides I don't know how anyone's going to know that it was us. It's something we can do very easily when no one is looking and no one else is around."

"I guess that kind of makes sense," Jill said. "But I don't know, as hilarious as this prank is it still seems kind of mean. I mean I have been in situations where I have been really desperate and I know that if something like this happened to me I certainly wouldn't appreciate it. As much as I would see the humor in the situation

I would still be pissed, no pun intended. Do you think I can have some time to think about it?"

Jack and James smiled and nodded. "Take all the time you need," Jack said. "You have a whole week to decide."

The three of them spent the rest of the afternoon just hanging out in the park. They didn't say anything else about their great locking the ladies room prank for the rest of the day, but Jill had to admit that she couldn't get the thought of it out of her mind. She was weighing all the options. On the one hand she couldn't deny that it would be absolutely hilarious and a great way to see lots of women desperate, but on the other hand, as a woman herself, she could see how incredibly mean it was and she knew that it could result in lots of people having accidents or suffering extreme bladder pain. But every time she thought of it she couldn't help but feel a tingle in her loins at the possibility and just how exciting it would be to witness, even to experience, if she wasn't such a chicken and had better bladder control.

Finally the day was winding down and they had to catch the bus back home and they didn't want to miss the bus because the bus only came by infrequently since the park was in an out-of-the-way area.

"I think I had better use the ladies room one last time before we get going," Jill said as she once again used the bathroom. As she was washing her hands at the sink she looked at the bathroom door and looked at the lock on the door. She made sure to look all around to make sure the coast was clear and as she was getting ready to leave she turned the door to locked, walked out of the bathroom and closed the door. When she turned it to open it again she found that it was clearly locked.

Jill went over to Jack and James with a big smile on her face as she saw a bunch of women walking towards the bathroom with distressed looks on their faces.

"What are you smiling about Jill?" Jack asked.

"I think that you guys are going to be proud of me," Jill said as she pointed to the women walking towards the restroom. "Just watch."

The three of them watched as the women approached the door to the bathroom and tried to open it only to find it locked. She saw one woman pounding on the door and looking really aggravated before cursing under her breath as the three women walked away looking disappointed.

"You didn't?" James said with a huge smile.

Jill smiled and nodded back. "I did!"

"Oh my God you actually did it!" James said. "High five!"

The three of them all high-fived each other as they looked at the three women walking away from the bathrooms, one waving her arms around in wild agitation.

"So does this mean you are in?" James asked.

Jill turned around and faced both of them as she nodded and smiled. "I am totally in!"

5

All that week Jill couldn't stop thinking and dreaming about what she had done to those three women at the park that weekend. She went back and forth through all sorts of different feelings. As she thought of the idea that those women wouldn't get to go to the bathroom she couldn't help but find herself getting extremely excited and even having to masturbate to thoughts of it. But then afterwards she started to feel really guilty and have second thoughts about it and wondered what those three women actually ended up doing after they found that the bathroom was locked.

Finally Jill could take it no more and she decided that she would blog about it as well as post a poll. She didn't say that this is what she actually did but posted it as a purely theoretical idea about the idea of locking a ladies room when three women were about to use it like that and whether it would be justifiable to do so.

When it was the day before the day of the big festival Jill checked the poll that she put on her website. Not surprisingly about 75% of the people who read her blog thought that it really was a hilarious idea and that she should go through with it.

When she checked the polls breakdown by gender not surprisingly more guys seem to be in favor of locking the ladies room than women were, but another surprising thing is that it wasn't by that big of a margin. Fully 50% of the women seemed to think that it was a hilarious idea as long as they weren't affected. Although most of the comments show that they would have been absolutely pissed, pun intended, if they had been on the receiving end of that. Lots of people posted nasty comments about the women wetting themselves and all this other stuff and some of the comments sounded a bit sadistic and mean.

But then Jill looked at some of the other comments and there was so much enthusiasm for the idea where she was being called brilliant and how this would be the most hilarious prank of all, and everyone was saying that if she ever had the chance to do that and she didn't take it she would be doing a disservice to all fans of desperation everywhere.

On the day of the big event the thoughts were still going through her mind even as she was going to the bathroom before leaving to meet the guys at the bus stop.

As the three of them got on the bus together they noticed that there were a lot of women on the bus who were guzzling down the liquids.

"Look at all these women drinking with no idea what awaits them," James said with an evil smirk as he laughed and ran his fingers together like some type of cartoonish super villain.

"Dude don't say it so loud," Jack said. "You sound like a super villain."

"Thank you, I was just thinking that!" Jill shouted.

"Hey you guys are both still on board with the plan aren't you?" James asked.

Jack nodded but Jill sat there looking indecisive.

"You're not getting cold feet on me are you?" James said.

"I don't know maybe this is just taking things too far," Jill said. "I mean we all like seeing people desperate but this seems like we are imposing it on lots of other people just for our own enjoyment. We could ruin the entire festival for all of these people just for our own sick amusement. Something about that just seems kind of wrong."

"It's not like we're going to kill anyone," James said. "Think of how hilarious this will be, seriously we will be like legends in the desperation community."

"I don't intend to broadcast our crime to the entire Internet," Jill said.

"You mean to say that you are going to go to this festival and watch all this desperation and not blog about it?" James said rolling his eyes.

"I didn't say that I would not mention that I encountered lots of desperation, I'm just not going to say that we were the ones who did it."

"What about that poll that you put on your website?" Jack asked.

"Oh, you saw that poll," Jill said forgetting that they were regular readers of her blog.

"I remember seeing that most people seemed to think that we would be insane not to go through with something like this," James said. "And I'm happy to say that I am sort of like the mastermind of this whole evil plan. Come on Jill, you have to realize just what a great opportunity this is. Stuff like this happens maybe once in a lifetime and again it's not like anyone's going to be hurt, their bladders perhaps, but I don't think anything horrible is going to happen if we do something like this."

"There are going to be like hundreds of people there," Jill said. "That's hundreds of people at a festival for pretty much the entire day drinking heavily without a bathroom. You don't think that some people are going to have accidents or that other people are going to try to hold and be in agony?"

"Well that's the whole fun part!" James said with a smirk.

"Yeah for you guys," Jill said. "But think of all those women who are going to have their entire day ruined just because of our little malicious prank here."

"Don't pretend that you're not going to be enjoying it as well Jill," James said. "Don't play so innocent. Besides we need you to be the one who locks the ladies room and makes it all come true. Don't bail out now; you're not chicken are you?"

"I am not going to give into peer pressure," Jill said.

James started bucking like a chicken and Jack burst out laughing.

"Dude what are you, like five years old?" Jack asked as he saw James making an idiot of himself as several people looked at them in the back of the bus. "Look if she doesn't want to do it maybe she has a point. Besides, we might see more desperation if we don't lock the ladies room. If the ladies room is in full operation a big line will likely develop around it and we can just sit there and watch from the tables all day long. Really if we lock the door no one is going to be standing up lining up at the bathroom. Sure people will be desperate all over the park but we are not going to see them standing in front of the bathroom to know that they have to go."

"I can't believe you guys are bailing on me," James said. "I'm sure we will see plenty more desperation if the bathrooms are locked all day. I understand that if we leave the bathrooms open it means we will see lots of desperate women all lining up in one spot, but they will be getting to go to the bathroom before they reached the bursting stage. If there are no bathrooms available for any of them all day long eventually every single woman at the festival will reach the stage where she is absolutely bursting. This festival continues for like what four, six hours. I think that the average woman has to go to the bathroom before that."

"I can absolutely attest to that fact," Jill said.

James nodded. "So you see by locking the bathroom we guarantee that almost every single woman at this place will be desperate at one point and eventually they will all be frantic. We won't have to wait for them to line up in one place as we can go anywhere in the park and see people crossing legs, hopping on 1 foot, desperately looking around for a bathroom. Come on you guys it will be total paradise. Plus I brought my video camera so that we are going to get the greatest footage and upload it all to the Internet. We will be absolute legends of female desperation. Hell we were going to lock the men's room too, so it's not like what we are doing is sexist, and we might even see some guys get desperate as well."

"I'm not really into seeing guys desperate," Jill said.

"Well again if you are lesbian you should look forward to the prospect of seeing so many women ready to burst."

"Yeah but male desperation is practically a myth," Jill said shaking her head. "Sure there are some guys who will never go to the bathroom outside under any circumstances, but I think that most of you guys if denied a place to pee will find a place to pee. If we lock the men's room and the ladies room I can assure you we will see lots of desperate women and relatively few desperate men. But we will see as lots of guys peeing on trees and that will just be even more agonizing for all the desperate women."

"Which is even more reason to do it!" James shouted. "I can't believe the two of you are so chicken and that you are bailing out on our brilliant and excellent plan, my plan really. Just think about it for the rest of the bus ride. We don't even have to do it right away; we have all day to think about it."

Jack and Jill nodded. "Okay," Jill said. "But let's not be unreasonable about this. We have to really think about this and all of the implications, that's the mature and responsible thing to be doing. There is such thing as having fun with desperation but then there is such a thing as taking it too far and I certainly don't want to be responsible for that."

"You don't have to be such a goody goody all the time Jill," James said. "Doing something a little bit evil so to speak is something everyone should try once."

"What you call being a goody-goody I call being considerate," Jill said turning her head away. "If you were ever a woman caught without a toilet for an extended amount of time you would understand that it's not all about just watching and viewing for your own pleasure. Sure it's nice to see desperation when it happens naturally, but to force it on people who aren't expecting it like that on a large scale, I think that that is just going too far."

"Okay but you might change your mind once we get there," James said.

The rest of the bus ride they didn't really say anything to each other. Jill could tell that the other guys were conflicted, or at least she could tell that Jack might have been persuaded by her argument. James kind of seemed like a bit of a Dick. Although the three of them shared the same interest they all shared different attitudes in regards to it, largely divided along gender lines. Jill had by far been more desperate herself than she had seen others desperate but having been in that position herself she could well sympathize with how cruel it could be to be denied a toilet when you really really want to go. And she was not into having accidents so she wouldn't want to cause anyone else to have an accident like that.

Finally after nearly an hour, owing to the traffic, the bus arrived at the park and by then Jill found that she already had to go to the bathroom. She was trying not to drink too much but she realized that when she was heavily facing a moral conundrum more deeply and thought about something she tended to get thirsty and drink more. She could already feel the tension growing in her own bladder.

"So are we going to go through with it?" James asked with a pleading look in his face.

"I think I need to use the ladies room," Jill said.

"Don't forget to lock the door!" James said.

Jill stuck out her tongue and went into the bathroom. There was one other woman in the bathroom with her and as she washed her hands at the sink after going to the bathroom she simply smiled and nodded at the other woman. When the other woman left Jill reached for the door handle and she could feel like all those characters in those old cartoon shows where they had a devil and an Angel, each on a different shoulder.

"Don't do it Jill, it would be wrong!" Jill's Angel said. "You have been in some of the worst desperate situations before and you know how terrible it is, even for people who enjoy the fetish occasionally."

"Don't listen to that namby-pamby," Jill's devil said. "Think of all these women in the park with their legs crossed dying to pee and getting to watch them squirm in agony all day. And you have a failsafe because you have the porta potty so nothing bad is going to happen to you. No one will ever know that you did it, it's the perfect crime."

Jill had never felt so conflicted before about any decision in her life. She thought that maybe she was making too much of it, this was a trivial thing, it wasn't like murder or anything, so a couple of people would have to pee, big deal. There were worse things in life after all.

Jill pushed in the button on the door to lock it but as she opened the door she saw a group of women coming including a mother who had three little girls with her as well as a little boy who was probably less than five years old and still too young to use the men's room by himself.

"Mommy I have to pee!" one of the little girls said as she jumped up and down hopping on 1 foot. Even at a young age like that little girls realize that you don't wait to go to the bathroom, Jill thought to herself.

As the group of women approached Jill held the door open for them and the mother and her desperate children ran into the bathroom.

"Thank you for holding the door open for us, you're such a nice young lady," the mother said as she piled her children into the bathroom.

Jill kept the door open and slowly walked out of the bathroom to see Jack and James standing there.

"Did you do it?" James asked.

"Guys I locked the door but I just couldn't bring myself to close it on that mother and her little children like that," Jill said. "That is something we have to consider, it isn't all just going to be adult women who should be able to control their bladders here, it's going to be mothers with their children and we don't want to make them desperate do we?"

"Don't worry I am sure that they will find some place to go," James said.

"I don't know I think maybe Jill has a point," Jack said.

"Oh come on you guys," James said. "You see one mother and a couple of bratty kids and all the sudden you want to throw away the plan of a lifetime?"

"Why don't we put it to a vote," Jack said. "I say that we abandon the plan and leave the ladies room unlocked. Besides, I'm sure as the park gets crowded we will see some really good lines if we just sit around here and wait for them."

"Well I say that we go through with the plan and become female desperation legends!" James said as he did some fist pumps and danced around.

"I'm sorry I just can't go through with it," Jill said. "I think I'm going to go back and unlock the door."

"Wait, Jill just let me argue this one more second," James said as he grabbed her arm.

Jill pushed his arm away. "No, I'm going to unlock the door; it's the right thing to do."

"Wait just hear me out!" James said as he and Jill started staring daggers at each other and that is when they heard a loud noise behind them.

When they turned around they saw the mother and her three daughters walking out of the restroom and standing there in front of the ladies room with his hand on the outside handle of the door slamming it shut was the little boy that was with them. He smiled as he skipped off following his mother and three sisters off into the distance.

James smiled and clapped. "Hallelujah it seems like desperation gods had a vote as well and they voted for divine intervention!"

6

Jack and Jill looked at each other and then they looked at James and then they looked at the little boy skipping off merrily with his family before looking back at the ladies room with the door now shut.

"Okay even I will admit that I tend towards atheism, but that was just freaking creepy!" Jack said.

"It's things like this that restore my faith that there is in fact a higher power and that it really likes to see women desperate to go to the bathroom," James said with a huge smile.

"Well if there is some type of higher power and they had some type of intelligent design when they were thinking of the male and female urinary systems respectively, then I would have to agree with you," Jill said. "But I can't believe this! What have I done?"

"Hey it wasn't your fault," James said. "It was the desperation gods!"

"Be serious here for a minute!" Jill said getting up in his face. "I was the one who locked the door, so it was my fault."

"Yeah but you were planning to unlock it right away," Jack said. "It was that little boy who closed the door."

"Yeah blame it on that little boy," James said.

"Although it's usually some type of boy to blame for female desperation, if I hadn't locked the door it wouldn't have mattered that he closed the door in the first place," Jill said shaking her head. "This is all my fault."

"Wait were there any other women in the restroom at the time?" Jack asked.

"No I'm pretty sure they all came out right before that mother and her children," Jill said. "I locked the door, oh my God, what have I done?"

"Jill, stop freaking out, it's not the end of the freaking world here!" James said.

"If you hadn't pressured me into this none of this would have ever happened!" Jill said.

"Wait, are you sure that you locked the door fully?" James said.

"I'm positive, I had the door locked, I held it open for that couple and then I came over here and started arguing with you guys and then the little boy came and closed the door. It's definitely locked."

That was when the three of them saw a group of three women coming over; they looked like they were in their late teens or early 20s, around the same age as them.

The first woman, a rather fit looking African-American woman, grabbed the handle to the bathroom and pushed it down and found that it wasn't opening and began pounding on the door. "Come on, I really have to go!" She began hopping up and down from foot to foot.

Jack, James and Jill all looked at her and looked at each other and exchanged guilty glances but all of them were still struggling to suppress a smile.

"Who the hell locks a bathroom on a busy day like today," the blonde woman next to her said.

"Is there any other bathroom around here?" the brunette woman next to her said.

"What's the matter?" Jill finally said as she came up behind the three of them.

"The damn bathroom's locked," the African-American woman said as she jingled the handle to find that it wasn't moving.

"Let me try," Jill said as she violently rocked the handle struggling in hopes that against all odds that if she just jiggled enough maybe the door would unlock itself. "It's not budging!"

"Let me try," the brunette woman said as she pulled on the handle and kicked the door. "God dammit, it's not budging for me either. It's clearly locked very tightly."

"Crap I really have to pee," the blonde woman said as she danced around in place as Jack and James tried hard to suppress snickering.

"I don't understand this bathroom was open just a few minutes ago," Jill said.

"But I think that this bathroom locks from the inside, which is pretty stupid if you ask me."

"Who the hell would lock it though?" the brunette woman asked.

"I don't know some dumb bitch," the African-American woman said as she once again pulled on the handle and pounded her fists on the door.

"Or maybe somebody just accidentally locked it without realizing what they did and the door blew shut or something like that," Jill said.

"Now what are we going to do?" the brunette said as she stood there tapping her foot.

"I'm so sorry," Jill said shaking her head.

"You don't have to apologize, it's not like it's your fault or anything," the African-American woman said. "But you'd think that they would design these things with more sense."

"Is there any other bathroom around here?" the blonde woman said.

That was when Jill suddenly thought of her secret hidden porta potty, her plan B, which could remedy this whole situation. She was about to say something but as she saw the three women standing in front of her, tapping their feet, crossing their arms and legs and hopping up and down, while she stood there with her bladder empty, something came over her.

Jill shrugged her shoulders and decided to say nothing. "No, I'm pretty sure that this is the only ladies room in the entire park."

"Fuck," the African-American woman said as she crossed her legs. "What are we supposed to do, go without a bathroom all damn day?"

"The people who plan these things are idiots," Jill said shaking her head.

"You know I couldn't help but overhear but I think that the men's room is still open," Jack said as he pointed to the men's room next door as men came in and out looking cheerful and relieved.

"Thanks just the same but men's rooms are pretty gross," the African-American woman said as her two companions sort of nodded. "But thanks for the offer. We will just go around and maybe we will find some bathroom somewhere."

"Good luck," Jill said as the three of them watched the three women waddle off looking rather frantic already with all day still to go.

"See wasn't that great?!" James said once the three women were out of distance.

"I don't know I kind of feel bad for them and I feel like I am responsible," Jill said while in the back of her mind she was thinking of that porta potty and thinking that she should run over to the three women and tell them about it.

"I told you Jill it was divine intervention from the bathroom gods or maybe goddesses, let's not be sexist, because women enjoy desperation too," James said as he winked at Jill like he was being some type of feminist superstar with that comment.

"I have to admit I did enjoy seeing that," Jack said. "And we offered to let them use the men's room so it's not like we didn't do anything or try to help."

"He's right, we were totally polite gentlemen," James said.

"Yeah right, you just wanted the girls to use the bathroom with you standing outside so that you can listen to them peeing!" Jill said.

"Hey are you saying that you never listen to girls peeing when you are in the restroom?" James asked.

Jill was taken aback by the comment as she had to admit she did enjoy listening to other women peeing in the restroom, especially after a really long hold when you could tell that they were desperate. "That's different; I'm supposed to be in there! You can't help but listen to other people peeing in the bathroom, so you might as well enjoy it while you are there!"

"Don't play so innocent, I noticed that you didn't mention your precious secret porta potty hidden away in the woods that they could have easily used," James said.

"Oh, I almost forgot about that, thanks for reminding me!" Jill said even though she knew well that she had thought about the porta potty while the three women were there. "It totally must have slipped my mind, but thank God I have that now because I don't know if I can go four or six hours without a bathroom."

"I am guessing you don't have as much of a problem with other women going 4 to 6 hours without a bathroom though," James said.

"You have to admit Jill you seemed to enjoy seeing those three women go off without relief just as much as we did," Jack said. "I don't always agree with everything that James said but he does kind of have a point. You are being a little bit hypocritical here."

"Look I really didn't want to lock the bathroom and I really regret doing it, but what is done is done and now we have to deal with it."

"Not you, because you have your precious porta potty," James said sticking out his tongue to which Jill did similar.

"Come on guys, let's be mature about this," Jack said. "Look the fact is the men's room is still open so if women get desperate enough that is always an option. So let's agree that we are not going to lock the men's room. Can we at least agree on that?"

James began laughing. "Sure, it's nice to have a place to pee! The urinals in the men's room are pretty nice, all eight of them."

Jill threw up her arms in frustration. "So once again the guys have a ton of places to pee and the girls come up short."

"Don't pretend that you aren't enjoying it," James said. "And that you aren't fully complicit."

"I thought that the desperation gods were behind it," Jill said as she stuck out her tongue.

"Well they played a role as well, you are in cahoots!" James said.

As the three of them stared at each other they suddenly burst out laughing.

"What are we laughing about?" Jill asked.

"The whole situation," James said. "This whole thing is absurd but I think that this really was like divinely ordained. Everything that has happened today suggests that this was supposed to happen. I believe that things happen for a reason and I believe that we are going to have a very interesting day ahead of us. Come on you have to admit that the whole thing is pretty hilarious."

Jill simply nodded. "Look I'm not made of stone, I feel bad about what has happened, but I can't deny that this is pretty hilarious. I mean that little boy just closing the door like that while we are in the midst of arguing, priceless."

"And those three women that we saw desperate and wanting for the bathroom getting turned away like that, they were hot!" Jack said.

Jill sort of blushed and nodded. "I'm not gonna lie, I was totally getting my lez on as those women got my motor running. But I still feel like I am complicit in the female urinary oppression of my sisters."

James laughed. "Female urinary oppression of my sisters, is there a special branch of feminism for that?"

Jill laughed back. "Sure, I'm the founding member, the high priestess. I think that we should perform a sacrifice to the bladder gods."

As the three of them were laughing they saw another group of women going over to the ladies room only to find the door shut and walking away looking angry and annoyed.

Jack, James and Jill watched the women walked past them and all began snickering and smirking before they burst out laughing.

"Hey guys I'm going to go get us some drinks, drinks are on me since Jill had the lady balls to lock the ladies room," James said and a couple of minutes later came back with a bunch of sodas.

The three of them all sat at the tables right by the bathrooms and for the next two hours or so the time flew by as they sat there drinking away as they watched woman after woman approach the restroom door only to walk away in various states of agitation, many cursing under their breath as the three of them tried to suppress their extreme laughter at what they had done. Every once in a while a woman would use the men's room but Jill noticed that James would frown every time a woman was bold enough to do so.

"Wow this soda goes right through me," James said. "I think that I need to use the bathroom."

"Yeah I think I need to go to," Jack said as the two of them stood up and went to use the men's room.

As Jill saw Jack and James go use the men's room she looked at her watch and was surprised it had been nearly 2 1/2 hours since they first arrived at the park. It had also been 2 1/2 hours since she last went to the bathroom and she noticed that the soda was going right to her bladder as well. For the first time she suddenly realized that she had to pee. She wasn't quite desperate yet, but had to go bad enough that she couldn't ignore the need and she knew it was time to go find the porta potty.

When Jack and James came back Jill stood up. "Guys I think that I need to use the bathroom."

"Didn't you hear, it's locked," James said as he and Jack burst out laughing.

"You guys know what I mean, it's time for me to go find that porta potty," Jill said. "Jack you know where it is better than I do so do you think you can maybe lead me there?"

"Sure, I know exactly where it is and I will take you right to it," Jack said. "Maybe I can even listen to you going!"

"Hey Jill, before you guys leave why don't we take a funny picture," James said. "Let's take a picture of Jill pulling on the door looking distressed."

"That's so silly you guys," Jill said.

"Come on don't you want something to remember this day by?" James asked.

Jill shrugged and they walked over to the restroom where she pounded on the door. "Oh no oh no it's locked and I really have to pee!" Jill said as she laughed as Jack and James snickered while taking pictures and videos of her posing in front of the ladies room door and pulling on it.

"Okay okay okay," Jill said. "Now I need to go pee for real."

"I think I'll just wait here, I can see a group of women approaching and I don't want to miss any of the action," James said.

"Shall we?" Jack said as he pointed off in the distance.

It was a rather long walk to the area where the porta potty was.

"This really is out of the way," Jill said looking at her watch. "It took us like 10 or 15 minutes to walk all the way over here. I better make this pee count so that I don't have to come back for a while."

As she approached Jack she saw him looking around like he was perplexed.

"Where is it?" Jill said. "Isn't it right around here or something like that?"

Jack rubbed his chin as though he were deep in thought. "I am positive that it was right over here."

"Are you sure?" Jill said as she suddenly felt her heart beating faster. "Are you sure this is exactly where it was?"

"I'm positive," Jack said. "We have been here a million times before and it's always right here."

"But it has to be here, it has to be!" Jill shouted.

"Calm down I'm sure it's right here," Jack said as he looked down and they realized that they were standing in the dirt that seemed to have an imprint about the size of a porta potty. "Or at least it was right here."

"Oh you are freaking kidding me," Jill shouted. "You promised it would be here!"

"Well it always has been before!" Jack shouted. "I guess someone must have come and taken it away."

"Holy crap!" Jill said as she began to panic. "Maybe they just moved it somewhere else?"

"No it's always right here," Jack said as he pointed to the dirt imprint beneath them. "This is pretty much is the spot and the end of the park. If it's not here it's just not here."

"Well let's keep looking for a little while," Jill said.

So for the next 15 or 20 minutes they walked around the whole area of the park but saw no sign of the porta potty.

"It's just not here Jill, I'm sorry, it's just not," Jack said.

"I can't freaking believe this!" Jill shouted. "You promised that it was always here and it has been here for year after year after year."

"Calm down," Jack said. "I know that you don't really like it but I guess that you'll just have to use the men's room."

"Gross," Jill said. "But I guess I have no choice. Let's just hurry and get back. If I had known this was going to happen I could've saved myself a half hour and just used the men's room in the first place."

Jack and Jill continued sprinting back to where the bathrooms were and that was when they saw James running towards them with a big smile on his face.

"Where the hell were you guys?" James asked. "You've been gone for more than a half-hour."

"We ran into some trouble," Jill said as she shot Jack an angry glance.

"Well you totally missed it," James said.

"Missed what?" Jack asked.

"Well there was this group of really desperate looking girls, like all of them super hotties and you could clearly see that they were all bursting like crazy and they had those bottles of water with them that Jill always carries around, so you know that they were probably tanking up on the liquids. Anyway they were going over to use the men's room and – "

"Let me guess you offered to let them use the men's room and then sat there and listened to them have loud hissy pees," Jill said as she raised her eyebrow at him and stuck out her tongue. "Pervert!"

James shook his head. "Nope, even better, I could see that these women were just dying out of their mind and the thought of them going to the bathroom was just unthinkably awful."

"Wait, what exactly did you do?" Jill said suddenly feeling more agitated.

James began laughing again. "Well you're going to think this is absolutely hilarious, and I know we said that we wouldn't but – "

"You didn't," Jack said as he looked at Jill, who looked at him and then looked at James.

"Please for the love of God say you didn't," Jill said as it suddenly dawned on her what they were getting at.

"When the desperate bitches were on their way to the men's room I ran ahead, walked into the men's room, and I totally locked the men's room!"

And that was the exact moment that Jill's world fell to pieces.

7

Jill felt almost like she was about to faint or something like that. Maybe she was just imagining it all, maybe this wasn't really happening, maybe she heard something wrong?

"I can't believe you did that!" Jack shouted at James. "I thought we agreed that we weren't going to lock the men's room."

James shrugged his shoulders. "I guess it slipped my mind. But dude if you had seen these hot women approaching you would have done the same exact thing, trust me." That was when he looked at Jill to see that she looked as white as a ghost. "What's your problem Jill?"

Jill's face went from white to suddenly very flush as an angry look came across her face and she punched James in the arm.

"What the hell was that for?" James said as he rubbed his arm. "Damn you hit pretty hard for a girl."

"Just be glad that I hit you on your arm and not somewhere else on your anatomy!" Jill shouted as she stomped her foot down.

"Damn Jill why are you so mad all the sudden? Are you on your period or something?"

Jill grabbed James by the shirt and looked him in the eyes. "How the hell could you lock the fucking men's room?! That was the one thing that we all agreed we wouldn't do!"

James pushed Jill off of him. "Okay so I locked the men's room what's the big deal? If you had seen these women trust me if you really are a lesbian you would have totally been lezing out over them. Trust me if you had been there you would have made the same decision and I just couldn't bear to see them getting relief in the men's room like that, it was infuriating, it was just plain not right.

Besides you've got your porta potty anyway."

"No she doesn't," Jack said shaking his head.

"What are you talking about?" James said. "Didn't you just go to the porta potty right now?"

Jack nodded. "We went to where the porta potty was the other day but I guess against all odds someone actually came and took it away. We looked around for it for like 15 or 20 minutes in the whole area but we saw absolutely no sign of it. It is completely and utterly gone."

James stood there, as they all stood there, silently for a minute as James let the information sink in before he burst out in roaring laughter.

"What the hell is so funny?!" Jill shouted.

"Oh man I wish I had been there," James said as he held his stomach as he continued laughing. "I wish I could have gotten a picture as the look on your face was probably priceless." He looked up to see that Jill was looking at him with a twitching face and that is when he took out his camera and snapped a picture. "That's a pretty good picture though too!"

"You bastard!" Jill shouted as she pushed him.

"Damn, touchy, all I did was take a picture!" James shouted as he dusted his shirt off.

"I'm not mad because you took a picture I am furious because you locked the one remaining restroom in the entire park!" Jill shouted.

James stood there staring at Jill for a minute as he let everything sink in. "Wait so you didn't get to go to the bathroom did you?"

"Noooooooooooooo," Jill said in a really agitated voice.

James snapped his fingers. "Oh snap, Jill has to pee, that's freaking hilarious!"

"This isn't funny!" Jill shouted. "Do I look like I am laughing?"

Jack couldn't help but force a smile. "Well to be fair Jill, it is kind of funny."

"What's funny about me having no place to go to the bathroom?" Jill said as she turned on him.

"Well," James said. "I mean this whole thing is kind of your fault in the first place so it's like that thing you always talk about in your blog that you are such a fan of, poetic something."

"You mean poetic justice?" Jill said subtly crossing her legs.

"Yeah that's it," James said as he once again snapped his fingers. "Poetic justice because you came here to see lots of women desperate, and now you are desperate yourself, the victim of your own prank."

"I didn't want to go through with it!" Jill shouted.

"You are still the one who locked the door," James said.

"Yeah but I didn't close the door, I was going to stop this whole thing at the beginning."

"I guess the desperation gods had other plans."

"Screw the desperation gods!"

"You shouldn't say that, you don't want to piss them off any more than they already are, no pun intended."

"Crap what am I going to do now?"

"How bad do you have to go?" Jack asked.

"Bad enough that I felt the need to use the bathroom over a half hour ago!" Jill shouted.

"Nice!" James said as he gave a thumbs-up to which Jill just stuck out her tongue.

"But it's not like a super emergency just yet is it?" Jack asked.

"I wouldn't say it's a super emergency brink of death desperation, but bad enough that I noticeably have to go."

"It's a nice look on you," James said with a smirk.

"Shut up!" Jack and Jill said simultaneously.

"I'm not about to die just yet," Jill said. "And you know that I have pretty good bladder control when I really have to, but I have to consider the long-term. We have already been here for three hours, three hours since I last went to the bathroom."

"I know I'd have to go," James said.

"You already went!" Jill snapped at him. "When is the soonest that the bus is going to arrive?"

"Well I think that the buses are running on sort of an unusual schedule today so I think that they probably won't be coming by until the whole festival is pretty much over, three hours from now."

"Three hours!" Jill said as she grabbed her hair and began pulling on it as she paced back and forth nervously. "Three freaking hours, and that's not even counting the bus ride home which could easily be an hour. What the hell am I going to do?"

"I don't know I guess you'll just have to hold it," James said with a laugh.

"Dammit it's not funny!" Jill shouted.

"Well Jill, I know you're pretty annoyed by this whole situation, and I know that you are justifiably mad at James right now, but you have to admit it's a little bit funny, at least a little bit don't you?" Jack said.

"You're taking his side?!" Jill said as she angrily pointed at James and once again crossed and uncrossed her legs.

"I'm not taking sides," Jack said. "I'm just saying you're always saying that we have to see things from your point of view and I think that we are seeing things from your point of view, even though you would like to deny it."

"What are you talking about?" Jill said as she tried to calm down and concentrate on holding her bladder.

"Well Jill think of it from our perspective, which I think is actually pretty close to yours," James said. "If you saw a girl bursting to pee and you knew that she was about a couple of hours away from a bathroom how would you feel, I mean if it were some other girl that you were watching?"

"Okay I'll admit that that would be pretty exciting," Jill said as she sort of started swinging her arms around and clapping her hands together while seeming to do some type of light breathing exercises. "But right now I have more practical concerns!"

"Again I'm not taking sides or anything," Jack said. "But I think you of all people would have to see the humor in this situation, can you at least give us that?"

"I guess so," Jill said as she sort of swung from side to side doing a little jitterbug.

"So come on, smile, laugh with us," Jack said as he began laughing as James began laughing as well. Eventually Jill started laughing along with them, even though she was still angry. "So is everything forgiven?"

Jill still looked angry but forced a smile. "Okay I guess I can see the humor in this. And I guess that if I weren't the one in the distressed and nervous position right now I would probably find this pretty funny. But the fact is I am in this situation, it's mostly your fault and I am pretty damn angry at it!"

"I realize that what I did was wrong," James said. "But can you understand at least why I did it?"

"Because you are selfish and inconsiderate," Jill said as she began tapping her foot in annoyance.

"Okay maybe I was a little bit selfish and inconsiderate," James said as he nodded. "And maybe when I let my fetish interests get the better of me I become a little bit oblivious. And I guess that you are sort of like our third conspirator and we didn't really take your needs into account. But again do you think you can see things from our perspective? Again I think it's pretty close to your perspective."

Jill looked at the two of them as they smiled really large as she stood there shifting from foot to foot. "Do you have to smile like that?!" Jill said as she was once again getting agitated.

James took out his camera and placed it on video.

"What are you doing now?!" Jill shouted. "And why are you smiling so much?"

"Well don't you want to document this entire thing for your blog later?" James said. "I mean this is a pretty harrowing epic right now. You are several hours from the bathroom, you have to pee really badly, you are clearly doing all of the motions. Do you have any thoughts that you would like to share?"

James put the camera up to her face and she felt really on the spot. She could hardly think about anything other than the fact that she desperately wanted to find a bathroom. "My name is Jill and I really really really have to pee!"

"When in the throes of desperation the desperate female often does various different types of ritual dances," James said as he continued videotaping Jill.

Jill couldn't help but smirk a little bit and begin laughing as she smacked her knees. "What is this like an anthropology video or something?!"

"In a time of great bladder distress the female animal will sometimes resort to cracking jokes trying to cloak the fact that she is deeply agitated and worried about the future," James said. "Watch as she nervously paces back and forth, shifting from leg to leg, trying to take all of the burning pressure off of her tiny little girl bladder."

"Hey I'll have you know that I probably have better bladder capacity than both of you guys combined!" Jill said as she stopped dancing. "You know what, enough of this videotape; I'm beginning to feel really self-conscious again."

James turned off the camera. "I'm sorry I just wanted to document this awesome situation."

"Awesome situation!" Jill shouted as she continued to jog in place and shift her legs around as she subtly put her hands in her back pockets and did a little squat. "What is so awesome about this? And why are you smiling and laughing so much?!"

"Sorry Jill we didn't mean to be total bastards and everything," Jack said. "I realize this is a serious situation, but you have to realize that it's hard not for us to be happy about the whole situation."

"What's there to be happy about?!" Jill shouted as she pressed her knees together and put her hands on top of them.

"Well we are two guys in a public place with a really desperate woman with us with no bathroom in sight for miles or hours and have no way out of the situation, why wouldn't we be excited?"

Jill was furious but she was trying to see things from their perspective. Situation reversed she couldn't deny that it must be a really exciting moment for them, but she was still completely enraged at the whole situation that was largely of their doing.

Jill breathed heavily. "I'm trying not to be mad and I'm trying to appreciate this whole situation from the perspective of a person who enjoys desperation. I realize that you guys are probably feeling all the blood rushing to certain parts of your anatomy that are controlling your brains right now. But I also want you to realize that I am in a seriously distressed situation and it is going to take all of my concentration and focus to get through the next couple of hours. So while you guys have nothing to do but watch and enjoy yourselves, I am going to be using all of my powers of focus and concentration to get through this situation unscathed. Do you guys understand?"

The two of them nodded.

"So now what do we do?" Jill asked.

"You know what since we were kind of jerks and this is sort of my fault drinks are on me!" James said as he took out a water bottle and squirted a large stream of water in Jill's general direction.

"That's it!" Jill shouted as she threw up her hands in frustration and started walking off.

"Jill where are you going?" Jack asked. "We wanted to spend the day with a desperate woman!"

"Well then start looking; I am sure that they are plenty around besides me thanks to you and your inconsiderate actions!" Jill said as she turned around before walking off.

"Where you going Jill?" Jack shouted again.

"I'm going to look for a bathroom!" Jill shouted back.

"But there are no bathrooms!" Jack shouted back.

"Don't remind me!" Jill shouted back.

"Wait Jill, come back!" Jack shouted as Jill continued walking with her backs towards them and held up her hands with middle fingers straight up.

"Damn she's pretty pissed off at us," James said. "Although I suppose it's better than her being pissed off on us!" James began bursting out laughing.

"Dude this is why she's leaving," Jack said. "You really are very inconsiderate when it comes to women; all you do is think with your Dick and only think about sex. If you had any consideration for Jill's feelings at all and saw her as anything other than light amusement and a sexual object, you would see this as more than an opportunity just to watch her wiggle and squirm and to see female flesh jiggling around."

The two of them turned around and they looked at Jill waddling off in the distance with her hands in her back pockets squeezing her ass and legs together and stopping every couple of paces to do a little squat and bend at the knees.

"Is it just me or does Jill just have an amazing ass?" James asked as the two of them stared.

"That's for damn sure," Jack said as the two of them watched Jill hobble off into the distance.

8

Jill stomped through the park not exactly sure where she was going. At the moment she didn't actually really care, she just knew that she wanted to be away from Jack and James. Although she kept trying to see things from their perspective and she felt somewhat bad about storming off, she just couldn't deal with being so visibly desperate for three hours in front of them. She knew that she would have to get back together with them by the time it was time to leave on the bus, but right now she just wanted some time to herself.

Surprisingly walking around helped to take her mind off of her bladder, as she walked slowly and listened to the sounds of nature around her she found it actually wasn't so bad being outside. She concentrated on feeling calm and centered.

After walking for a while she got thirsty and took out her bottle of water but then she remembered that it was still several hours before she would get to a bathroom so she only took the smallest sips here and there, just enough to keep herself hydrated and to keep her mouth moist.

After walking around for a while she did find herself becoming calmer and to some degree the feeling of desperation went into remission a little bit and she began to calm down even further. She looked at her watch to see that there was still about 2 1/2 hours to go until they had to catch the bus. She found herself looking at her watch every five minutes and it seemed like time slowed down the more she had to go to the bathroom.

"God dammit James!" she shouted. She had indeed walked around pretty much the entire park and there wasn't any sign of a bathroom or a porta potty or anything like that. It was indeed totally gone and as she contemplated that she thought that maybe the guys were right. To some degree she was responsible for locking the door so maybe it really was poetic justice what was happening to her now. At least she would have plenty to blog about when she got home and she had to admit that the feeling of a full bladder did arouse her. She was kind of angry that she couldn't deny that on some level it was an exciting feeling to be desperate outside far away from a bathroom. She hated herself for enjoying it for that brief moment even though that is what she came here to do.

"You can do this Jill, you've done it before," she kept saying to herself. Granted those other times she managed to hold for such a long stretch of time were at home where she was testing her limits but with the toilet safely a few feet away and even then it was quite maddening, but at least it was all very private.

As she continued to circle the park realizing the futility of continuing to look for a bathroom she wondered how many other people were in a similar situation to her. She could see that several people were playing all sorts of ballgames and sitting around the table still drinking in spite of the fact that they must have known by now that there were no bathrooms available.

Then she saw a bunch of kids playing with water pistols squirting them all around. One little kid even came up and began squirting her with it.

"Hey stop that you little brat!" Jill shouted.

"What's your problem lady?" the little kid said as he continued squirting his gun around.

"It's inconsiderate to go around squirting people with liquids like that without their permission."

What was it about men who just love to freely squirt around their liquids like that, Jill thought to herself. Seeing that certainly wasn't helping her situation.

That was when a little girl came over and stared at Jill.

"Is something the matter little girl?" Jill said as she shifted from leg to leg.

"I don't know what her problem is," the boy said as he ran around squirting his pistol in all different directions.

The little girl began giggling like crazy as she pointed at Jill.

"What is so funny little girl?" Jill said still shifting from leg to leg and shaking her leg a little bit as she subtly crossed herself.

That was when the girl gave Jill an evil look of recognition that seemed especially malevolent coming from a young child like that.

"You've got to pee!" the little girl said as she cackled like an evil banshee.

"What are you talking about?" Jill said not even realizing that she was bending at the knees and that her legs were shaking.

"You're doing the pee dance!" the girl said as all the boys began smiling and laughing.

"I am not!" Jill said as she stood perfectly still.

"Pee dance! Pee dance! Pee dance!" all the kids began chanting as they pointed at Jill.

"You know it's not polite to point and stare at people like that," Jill said. She couldn't believe that even at a young age this little girl managed to recognize the signs. It really was quite embarrassing.

"Why don't you just pee?" the little girl said.

Jill really didn't want to be having this conversation with a group of little children.

"Unfortunately some idiot locked all the bathrooms," Jill said.

"Why not just pee on a tree then?" one of the boys asked as the rest of them nodded in agreement.

"Ladies can't just whip it out and tinkle on a tree," Jill said.

"I do!" the little girl said as she smiled. "I do it all the time, I just squat and go. Why don't you just squat on a tree?"

Now Jill was really infuriated but trying not to show her anger. It infuriated her that this little girl knew how to squat and relieve herself outdoors in a way that Jill was never taught.

"It's not ladylike to just pee on a tree like that," Jill said. "Can't you children ever learn to hold it?"

"It's easier just to pee," one of the boys said as everyone nodded in agreement.

"Well when you are adults you will realize it's not appropriate to just go to the bathroom wherever you feel like it, that's what dogs do," Jill said desperately wishing right now that she was a dog.

The kids all looked at each other before one of the boys spoke. "Being an adult sucks! Pee dance! Pee dance!"

As all of the kids began chanting Jill ran off once again. Now she was feeling extremely humiliated, even little kids were able to find relief when she wasn't, but they hadn't yet been filled with society's taboos about outdoor urination.

She continued to pace around the park looking at all the people and imagining how desperate they could be. She didn't see that many signs of visible desperation but maybe like her they were trying to hide it. Normally she was able to hide it but as she walked around she couldn't help but stop every couple of minutes to bend or to cross her legs or to grab herself.

That was when she saw a bunch of guys walking around throwing cans of soda or beer on the floor.

"I really have to piss!" one of the guys said as Jill's ears perked up.

"All the bathrooms are locked," one of the other guys said.

"I know someplace we can piss," another one of the guys said.

Could it possibly be, could they know about some hidden bathroom somewhere that she didn't know about? She had to find out, so she tried to follow them without making it look like she was stalking them. She just sort of walked slowly behind them until they came to the area where the porta potty was.

"I guess I wasn't the only person who knew about Plan B," Jill said as she lamented the fact that the porta potty was a no-show.

"It looks like the porta potty is gone, but we can just piss in the sand here," the guy said as the guys all took positions around and began peeing on trees and bushes and in the dirt.

"Oh my God!" Jill said as she ran away not wanting to see all those guys relieving themselves. Now she had to pee worse than ever. What was it about knowing that others were gaining relief when you weren't that made your own desperation so many times worse?

Jill checked her watch and it had now been at least four hours since they arrived, four hours since she last used the bathroom and at least another two hours to go until the bus was going to arrive.

"Oh Christ I am never going to make it," Jill said as she crossed her legs and put her hands between her knees.

"Excuse me?" said a female voice behind Jill, startling her. She turned around to see standing there was an absolutely drop dead gorgeous little Asian girl who was standing there with a smile. Jill couldn't believe how attractive the girl was and it was like her ultimate lesbian fantasy come to life. Now she was feeling more self-conscious than ever!

"Hey!" Jill said trying to maintain her composure but undeniably shifting from one leg to the other.

"Hi my name is Kimmy," she said as she stuck out her hand which Jill shook.

"I'm Jill," Jill said. "What can I do for you Kimmy?"

"I feel kind of shy about asking this," Kimmy said. "But you know where the ladies room is?"

Jill stared at Kimmy and that was when she noticed that Kimmy also had her knees pressed together and her hands on her knees with her bare legs exposed and clearly shaking.

Jill couldn't help but laugh. "You have to go too, huh?"

Kimmy nodded. "I haven't gone all day and I have to go really really bad. All that soda really goes right through me."

"I know what you mean I feel ready to burst."

The two of them stood there for a moment staring at each other before Jill finally spoke. "Unfortunately it seems like they locked the restrooms, and it figures they would lock them on the day of the biggest event of the year where everyone is drinking a whole lot."

"Well that was stupid," Kimmy said.

"Totally."

"So now what are we going to do?"

Jill shrugged her shoulder. "I don't know, I haven't gone in four hours and I have just been kind of holding it."

Suddenly Kimmy had a really big smile on her face. "Do you like holding it?"

"Do I what?" Jill asked suddenly taken aback by the question.

Kimmy sort of blushed. "I know this is going to sound silly but sometimes I kind of like the feeling of holding it in, know what I mean?"

Jill did know what she meant, all too well. She couldn't believe this, was this girl actually interested in desperation?

"What do you mean?" Jill said, trying to play dumb.

"I hope I don't sound like I'm some type of weirdo or something like that but sometimes when I get a really full bladder it's just sort of like a really nice feeling, you know, down there in your lady parts."

Now Jill was going out of her mind. Here was this gorgeous Asian girl totally into desperation but she was feeling too shy to admit how excited she was.

As Jill stood there with her legs tightly crossed she slowly raised her hand

and put it on Kimmy's shoulder and smiled. "I understand totally."

As the two of them stood there practically shaking with desperation that was when they knew that there was sort of an unspoken understanding between them.

It took her a moment to choke out the words but finally Jill said what she was thinking. "You know I think a girl can look pretty cute when she has to go to the bathroom." She couldn't believe that she said it but this was a golden opportunity, no pun intended.

That was when Kimmy's face lit up like she had just found the lost city of gold.

"Me too!" Kimmy shouted. "I thought I was the only one."

"You're not the only one, trust me," Jill said smiling as she crossed her legs.

The next thing that happened was totally unexpected as Kimmy leaned forward and kissed Jill on the lips. The two of them pulled back before continuing. Although she knew she was a lesbian since her late teen years Jill had never actually kissed a girl before so this was a new experience for her that temporarily took her focus off of the time bomb that she felt was about to go off in her bladder.

Then Kimmy pushed back.

"What's wrong?" Jill asked.

"I know I said that I really like the feeling of having to pee," Kimmy said as she danced from foot to foot. "But I really really have to go, like super incredibly bad!"

"So do I?" Jill said as she bent at the knees. "But I guess there is nothing we can do, the bathroom is closed."

"I know a place we can go," Kimmy said as she waved Jill ahead.

"Where are we going? I looked all over the place, there isn't any bathroom, not even that porta potty that used to be here," Jill said.

"You'll see," Kimmy said as the two of them slowly hobbled over to some trees.

"I don't see a bathroom here," Jill said and that was when she saw Kimmy was pulling at her skirt and that was when Jill noticed what was going to happen as her bladder shuddered at the thought.

"Can you just make sure no one comes while I am going," Kimmy said as she pulled down her panties and began squatting.

"Sure," Jill said as she stood in front of Kimmy with her back towards her.

"You can watch if you want," Kimmy said as Jill's entire body began trembling.

"What was that?" She said turning around.

"I don't mind an audience," Kimmy said as Jill turned around and watched as a golden stream started hissing out between Kimmy's legs and into the dirt on the floor in front of them. It was simultaneously the most beautiful and most torturous scene that Jill had ever witnessed in her entire life. Just when it seemed like the stream was stopping it then started up again. It seemed like she was peeing forever and ever and Jill could feel her eyes become watery with tears as she witnessed this fountain of urine gushing out of this girl like a firehose as she moaned with relief.

Finally Kimmy finished and pulled up her panties and stood up with a huge smile on her face. "I feel so much better!"

"You weren't kidding, you really had to go!" Jill said as the two of them laughed. "So I guess now that that is taken care of we should get going."

"I thought you had to pee."

"Of course I do!" Jill said as she danced back and forth. "Really really bad, like insanely bad."

"Then why don't you go?" Kimmy said.

"When you said that you had a place I was assuming that you knew where there was a bathroom."

"We're out in the middle of nowhere; all of nature is a bathroom."

"Yeah, if you're a guy!"

"I don't think that I look like a guy do you?" Kimmy said as she stuck out her tongue.

"No you are all woman," Jill said as she danced back and forth clearly more frantic than ever.

"Then why don't you pee like I did?"

Jill sort of blushed. "You see the thing is I was never taught how to go to the bathroom outside. I don't know how to squat without falling over on my ass and peeing all over myself."

"Well you just pull down your pants and – "

"I think the only way I could possibly go to the bathroom without getting pee all over myself is if I took off my pants and panties altogether and just stood with my legs apart and peed like that."

Kimmy smiled and began giggling. "Okay go ahead, I'll stand watch."

"I'm not going to get half naked in the middle of the park like this when people could come by and see!"

"So you are shy?"

"Very much so."

Kimmy smiled. "That's pretty cute."

"You think so," said Jill very visibly blushing.

"You do a really nice pee dance Jill!"

"Thank you," Jill said as she continued shifting from leg to leg and bending at the knees. "I really really really have to go."

"And yet you won't just go pee right now?"

"I would, but I can't!" Jill said as she grabbed herself as Kimmy smiled even larger.

"So you are just going to keep holding it?" Kimmy said as her eyes started lighting up with joy and Jill began shaking at the legs.

"I guess I don't have much choice."

"But the bus won't arrive for another hour and a half and then it could be an hour before we end up getting home. Are you really going to hold it all that time?"

Jill nodded very rapidly as she continued to hop from 1 foot to another. That was when Kimmy came and hugged Jill tightly and shrieked with joy. "This is the happiest day of my life!" Kimmy shouted.

"Really?" Jill said as Kimmy continued hugging her.

"I always wanted to find a really cute girl who liked desperation and now I found one who has no possibility of using a bathroom for the next 2 1/2 hours. This is going to be the best 2 1/2 hours of my life!"

As Jill stood there with her legs crossed tightly and her hands between her legs with a smiling Kimmy standing there watching her Jill had to admit that she had never been more turned on and she knew that whatever else happened today it would indeed be the most interesting couple of hours of her life.

9

Kimmy and Jill spent the next half hour just walking around as Jill started to stop every couple of minutes to grab herself. Kimmy gave her words of encouragement and Jill liked all the attention she was getting from this attractive girl but she had to admit that she wasn't sure how much longer she could hold it.

"Look at her she looks pretty desperate!" Kimmy said pointing to another woman who was shifting from foot to foot. "Probably not as much as you though Jill." Kimmy kissed Jill on the cheek causing her to blush.

During all this time Jill and Kimmy kept their hands held together and Jill kept squeezing Kimmy's hand harder and harder as she had to pee more and more.

"I think I really need to sit down," Jill said as she began to hobble and shake. "I can't remember ever having to pee this badly before. Maybe if we go back to the area where the bathrooms are maybe someone will have through some miracle unlocked them."

"I hope not," Kimmy said as she burst out laughing as Jill laughed feebly but Kimmy could see that Jill was desperate on a truly epic scale.

Slowly Kimmy walked Jill over to the area by where the bathrooms are. They approached the ladies room only to find that it was locked, then approached the men's room to find that it was similarly locked.

"Dammit dammit dammit!" Jill said as she pounded on the door to the ladies room. "Why did I ever do this?!"

"Do what?" Kimmy asked as she looked at Jill.

"Drink so much," Jill said to avoid admitting that she was the one who locked the bathroom. But as the two of them were standing there that was when she saw the people that she didn't quite want to see at that moment. It was Jack and James walking over towards them. "Oh no," Jill said under her breath.

"What's wrong?" Kimmy asked.

"It's my jerk-ish friends," Jill said. "I don't want them to see me like this."

"Jill where were you all this time?" Jack asked. "We were worried about you."

"How's the bladder?" James said as he laughed loud.

"She has to pee really bad!" Kimmy said giggling.

"Who's the lovely lady Jill?" James asked.

"This is my friend Kimmy," Jill said as she crouched over trying to relieve the pressure on her bladder.

"I like to think of us as more than friends," Kimmy said as she patted Jill on the ass and gave her a pinch causing her to blush profusely and also grab herself to keep control of her bladder.

"Well it looks like Jill got some lesbian action!" James shouted. "If I did that to her she would have slapped me!"

"You would have deserved it too!" Jill shouted.

"Hey I hope you are still not mad at me," James said. "Besides it's all your fault anyway, this is what you get for locking the bathroom."

"What?" Kimmy said as she looked at Jill standing there shifting from foot to foot in front of the locked ladies room. "Jill, were you the one who locked the bathrooms?"

"Not exactly," Jill said as she gritted her teeth. "It's a complicated story."

"The desperation gods helped a bit," James said.

"You guys like desperation too?" Kimmy said smiling. "Did you really lock the bathroom just to create all this desperation?"

"It was an accident, I locked the door and then some kid closed the door but then James had to be an idiot and lock the men's room and I was supposed to have a porta potty that I could go to but then the porta potty was removed and it's all just been so crazy," Jill said as she calmed down and explained to Kimmy everything that happened.

"That is so freaking bad ass!" Kimmy shouted as she patted Jill on the back causing Jill to grab herself tightly and moan. "Sorry."

"I really didn't mean for things to spiral out of control like this," Jill said as she stood there trembling.

"But if they hadn't we never would have met," Kimmy said. "Aren't you glad all of this happened?"

"You have to admit that things did go pretty well Jill," James said. "We got a whole day of viewing desperate women, you met a cute new friend and we still have another 45 minutes before the bus arrives!"

"Oh my God I'll never make it!" Jill said as they helped her to sit down.

"I have to admit Jill you are pretty bad ass for going through with this," Jack said. "So we are going to help you get through this."

"You will?" Jill said as she sat down with her legs tightly crossed tapping her feet a hundred miles a second.

"Sure we will, we are your friends Jill," James said." Just because we are enjoying every second of your agonizing desperation doesn't mean that we don't care. You have made this the most entertaining day of our lives."

"Totally," Kimmy said as she kissed Jill on the cheek as Jack and James made all sorts of hooting and hollering noises.

So the three of them sat down together with Jill on one side and the other three of them on the other side of the table all smiling at her and James took out the video camera.

"Do you have anything to say to your millions of adoring fans in the desperation community Jill?" James said.

Jill sat there and they could still hear her feet tapping a hundred miles a second as she choked out something that they couldn't hear.

"What was that, we couldn't hear you Jill," James said.

"All things are better in moderation!" Jill said as the four of them began laughing. "I knew I shouldn't drink anything but I am so thirsty."

Kimmy picked up a bottle of soda and offered it to Jill but she put up her hands and shook her head.

"How about we make a deal Jill?" Kimmy said with a very evil smirk.

"A d-deal," Jill said as she tapped her fingers nervously on the table.

Kimmy took out a coin. "If the coin is heads you just take a small tiny sip, but if it's tails you drink a whole bottle."

"Holy Shit," James said. "Do it Jill! Don't chicken out right now."

"I don't know," Jill said as she leaned back on her seat and looked up at the sky like she was about to scream.

James began making clucking chicken noises as he started dancing around the table flapping his arms.

"Oh fuck it give me that," Jill said as she took the soda and began guzzling it down until she had finished the entire thing and slammed it down on the table as the three of them clapped. As Jill looked at the empty bottle of soda and burped she covered up her mouth and looked ahead like she just smashed the 10 commandments. "What have I done?!"

Jill spent the next couple of minutes just chatting casually with her friends trying to hide the fact that she was desperate but they could all feel the table shaking from Jill tapping her feet and shaking her legs.

"Damn Jill this is going to register on the Richter scale soon," Jack said as they all felt the table shaking.

"I can't help but I have to go so bad!" Jill said as she stood up and started dancing around. "Maybe if I stand up it will take some of the pressure off."

"I think we had better start walking over to the bus stop anyway," Jack said. "We certainly don't want to miss the bus."

As the four of them stood at the bus stop they looked around to see several other women shifting from leg to leg and they couldn't help but smirk and snicker. Of all of them Jill looked like she was the most frantic of all. Finally the bus pulled up and all of the passengers slowly got on board and they could see several of the women were sitting down very slowly to avoid jostling their bladders.

"Come on people let's get seated!" the bus driver shouted.

The three of them got seats in the middle of the bus. Jack and James took the seat in front of Kimmy and Jill.

"It should only be another 45 minutes to an hour before we get home, do you think you can make it Jill?" Jack asked.

"Well I'm certainly going to try," Jill said with her eyes watering. "But I've never had to go so badly before."

"Don't worry Jill I believe in you," Kimmy said as she put her hand on Jill's trembling leg and began running her fingernails up and down which was making Jill excited but also relaxing her a bit.

As Jill sat in the seat shaking like crazy and tapping her feet loudly they could hear other people on the bus complaining that they had to go to the bathroom really bad which caused Kimmy, James and Jack to all smile, but Jill was too desperate to even pay attention.

"Hey Jill," Kimmy said as she ran her fingers through Jill's hair.

"Yeah?" Jill said still shaking in her seat.

"I had a real lot of fun today and I am wondering if you would like to come back to my place for the night, you know for coffee," Kimmy said smiling.

"I don't think I can drink anymore right now," Jill said tightly crossing her legs and grabbing herself in her seat.

"She wants to have sex with you numbskull," James said really loudly as people around them looked at them and Jack punched James in the arm telling him to shut up.

Kimmy started to burst out laughing before turning to Jill. "If we are going to go to my place we just have to get off at the next stop. We will have to wait at the bus stop for a couple of minutes and then we will get back on the next bus and then it's just a few minutes to my house. So what do you say?"

"Go for it Jill," James said. "You've earned it."

"Okay," Jill said. "But I hope I make it."

"I'm sure there is probably a bathroom at the bus station," Jack said.

Kimmy frowned. "You know I think you are right."

"I guess I can catch a ride back to my place tomorrow," Jill said. "You guys can go on without me right?"

"Sure," Jack said.

"Well this is pretty much our stop then," Kimmy said as the bus slowed to a stop.

As the two of them stood up James stood up as well. "Look Jill I realized that I was a bit of a jerk this whole day and I just want to say that I am sorry for everything and you are the ultimate bad ass of female desperation."

"Thank you," Jill said as she put her arm around Kimmy and pulled her close. "But I think things worked out pretty well."

Kimmy and Jill got off of the bus as Jill raced towards the bathrooms but several women were in front of them in line. Kimmy was waiting in front of Jill.

"Do you think maybe I can cut in line?" Jill asked Kimmy.

"I kind of had a lot to drink," Kimmy said to which Jill simply nodded. As badly as she wanted to go to the bathroom she knew how much Kimmy was enjoying this.

As Kimmy went into the bathroom Jill stood outside of the bathroom door hopping from foot to foot and noticed that Kimmy was taking her sweet time. Finally the door opened and Kimmy sort of slipped out really quickly and closed the door. Jill turned the knob on the door and found that it wasn't budging.

"What's the matter Jill?" Kimmy asked with an evil smirk on her face.

"It's locked!" Jill screamed as he banged on the door. "I can't believe it it's locked. Oh my God you didn't?"

Jill turned to Kimmy who simply smiled and shrugged her shoulders. "Oops, what are the odds?"

"All aboard!" the announcement came as they saw the bus pulling up.

"What the hell do you think you're doing?" Jill said as she hobbled towards the bus with Kimmy helping to hold her up.

"For what I've got planned you need a full bladder," Kimmy said as Jill grabbed herself tightly and slowly sat down on the bus.

"I don't know if I'm going to make it," Jill said. "It's been over seven hours since I went to the bathroom; I think this is a record for me."

"It is a magical evening," Kimmy said as she patted Jill on the back. "Don't worry it will all be worth it."

A short time the bus arrived and Kimmy stood up and offered her hand to Jill to help her up. "This is our stop."

Kimmy held Jill's hand as she led her down the hallway and opened the door to her room.

"Here we are!" Kimmy said as she turned the lights on revealing a rather nice looking dormitory. "And we have the place all to ourselves because my roommate's gone for the weekend."

"Kimmy I think I'm about to wet myself!" Jill said squeezing her legs tightly together and grabbing herself.

"Then you had better get undressed," Kimmy said with another evil smirk.

"What?" Jill said as she stood there trembling.

"Take it off bitch!" Kimmy shouted as she smacked Jill on the ass and laughed hysterically.

Jill was so turned on that she didn't even question what was going on. First she took off her shirt and bra and threw them on the floor as Kimmy sat there clapping. Then she pulled down her pants and panties and threw them to the side. She was now standing there fully naked and holding her achingly full bladder and trying to cover up her breasts with the upper part of her arms as she could feel the goose pimples all over her body.

"I've never been seen naked like this before," Jill said whimpering as she held her bladder.

"It's a good look on you!" Kimmy said as Jill continued dancing in place.

"So what happens now," Jill said as she continued trembling even more as now she was trembling both from the humiliation of being desperate and the humiliation of being naked.

Kimmy came over and began passionately making out with Jill and caressing her backside causing little spurts of urine to come out from between her legs.

"I'm sorry," Jill said. "I don't think I can hold it anymore."

"Come over here," Kimberly said as she pushed Jill down on her bed, took out a pair of handcuffs and before Jill knew what happened she was handcuffed to the bed.

Kimmy climbed on top of her, her skirt brushing against Jill's naked body and causing her to shudder. "I bet you're ticklish!"

"I think that I'm a little bit ticklish – "Jill started saying as Kimberly started running her fingernails up and down Jill's body causing her to shriek like a banshee and let out more drops of pee that were splattering all over Kimmy's skirt. She continued tickling Jill until she completely lost control soaking the bed and giving her the most explosive orgasm of her life.

"So how do you feel Jill?" Kimberly said as she sat on top of Jill's naked body, still fully dressed caressing her breasts with her long nails.

"I'm really glad that I held it," Jill said. "I also feel that I am a lot more ticklish than I thought I was."

Kimmy smiled. "That's good."

"It is?" Jill said as she breathed heavily, her breasts heaving up and down.

Kimmy nodded again. "Yep, because you are handcuffed, naked and I don't have anything to do for the next couple of hours!"

"Wait, Kimmy!" Jill shouted but before she could say another word she could feel Kimmy's fingernails assaulting every inch of her body.

The next few hours after that were kind of a blur.

Epilogue

The next morning Jill woke up in bed next to Kimmy whose fully clothed body was still lying on top of Jill in her urine soaked bed and Jill felt completely exhausted like she never had before in her entire life.

Eventually Kimmy woke up running her fingers through Jill's hair and kissing her on the lips.

"Did you have a good night?" Kimmy asked.

Jill nodded and smiled as she squirmed around a little.

"Is something the matter?" Kimmy said as she ran her fingernail over Jill's nipple.

"Kimmy," Jill said licking her lips.

"Yes?" she said as she continued running her fingers through Jill's hair.

"I haven't gone to the bathroom all night and I really really have to pee!"

Kimmy continued circling her fingernail around Jill's nipple as she smiled really large, kissed Jill on the lips, came up and looked her in the eye. "Hold it!"

At the end of the day Jill could barely stand up and although her bladder was still in a tremendous amount of pain and soreness that would probably last her for a good long while, she had never felt more satisfied. She slowly limped out of Kimmy's bed and Kimmy helped her into the shower and they showered together, then she helped Jill get dressed and led her to the bus stop.

"Email me," Kimmy said as Jill got on the bus.

"Maybe next time you can get naked and hold it," Jill said as she winked at Kimmy.

"Maybe," Kimmy said. "Although I liked the way things were this time just fine!"

Jill wasn't one to argue so she nodded and got on the bus. Within a short time she got back to her dorm still feeling completely physically drained but she decided to go on the Internet to see if there was anything about the festival online. She came up with several articles saying how the bathrooms were all locked and how hundreds of people were peeing all over the place and having accidents and there was lots of pictures and videos and everything, including a video that she saw that James uploaded of her that had tons and tons of likes. She noticed that one of the people commenting was familiar. It was from Barbara who said with great enthusiasm "I know that girl!"

As Jill looked at the videos of her making rounds on the Internet she had to admit that she felt extremely embarrassed and self-conscious, but looking at all the comments that said she was a bad ass made her feel quite satisfied.

Jill went to her blog, sat down and began to write.

The Great Locked Ladies Room Caper, Chapter 1.

<u>Some Words from the Author</u>

I feel that this novella is a little bit of autobiographical but only a little bit. The main female protagonist in the story, Jill, is based entirely off of me and she has all the same attitudes towards going to the bathroom and desperation that I do, not to mention the same name! Like me she is a lesbian who is attracted to Asian women, who enjoys female desperation, both watching and experiencing, has her own desperation blog, cannot go to the bathroom outdoors and generally finds it extremely frustrating when she is unable to go to the bathroom and others are, that being both a pet peeve and a primary turn on.

Beyond that this story is entirely fictional, although there were several real-life influences on the formation of this novella. For one thing growing up I was shy and socially awkward and most of my friends turned out to be guys, mostly guys I knew through family and other friends. So there were very many occasions during which I would be the only girl in a social group and find myself quite desperate when it came time to use the bathroom! Trips outside were of course the worst because the boys would always be able to just go pee on a tree while I would just have to cross my legs and grit my teeth until we got home.

Even in situations where bathrooms were available the guys would frequently be able to go without any waiting whatsoever while the line to the ladies room was well out the door, and then sometimes you cave into peer pressure and you agree that you will just wait until you can find another bathroom, however long that might be, and it might be quite a while! So meanwhile the guys have gotten to go to pee and you are sitting there with your legs crossed trying not to complain but ready to scream your head off!

I have never experienced a locked ladies room at a park before like in the story although I have experienced situations where the ladies room was locked, whereas the men's room was entirely open, but I would dare not use it because I just did not have the guts to do so, it was always a taboo for me and one that I was unwilling to break. Though if it was a choice between using the men's room and having an accident I probably would choose to use the men's room, although fortunately I have never had to make that decision before, although I have been seriously tempted as I am sure that most women have at some point in their lives and many will give into that temptation! I certainly can't blame anyone who would.

I have had cases where I have been at a park and been unable to find a bathroom which again was frustrating because the boys could just go pee out in a field somewhere or on a tree. And I have had cases where the ladies room was locked at some of the worst of times. The worst case was when I was on a long bus trip to Washington DC where we only had one brief 15 minute rest stop to use the restroom about two hours into a four hour journey, and of course the ladies room was locked so I ended up having to hold it for the full four hours. By the time that bus finally pulled in all the women stormed off the bus and there was a gigantic line like 60 women long for like two or three stalls that was probably about 45 minutes long. I was practically ready to explode by the time I finally got to go to the bathroom and I can still remember the back of the head of the Muslim girl standing in front of me in line for those 45 minutes over 20 years later! So yeah, when you are that desperate and you have nothing else to distract you, you remember these types of things.

I have noticed that it seems like the ladies room is more likely to be out of order than the men's room is a lot of the time. My theory is that since there are fewer stalls and everything in the ladies room if one of them is clogged they might end up shutting down the entire bathroom, whereas the men's room would still have urinals available to use. But as one guy also pointed out to me you never see a men's toilet clogged by female sanitary products, and I have to admit that that's probably a good point. Bathrooms always tell you not to flush those type of products down the toilet, but of course people are inconsiderate and stupid and don't listen, and as a result we end up with situations where now no one gets to use the damn bathroom!

Even worse was in high school where I experienced a full year or two of fairly regular desperation. There was a situation at our school where they found drugs and alcohol being hidden in one of the girls restrooms, so of course they decided to punish everyone for the actions of a few. They didn't lock every single bathroom, because obviously then people would complain or view it as some type of human rights violation, but they did close all of the ladies rooms except for the one by the nurses office. My school had about 1500 students and if you assume an equal number of boys and girls that would equal about 750 girls for one bathroom with five stalls, which results in one toilet per 150 girls. The bathroom by the nurses' office was in sort of an out-of-the-way area so of course even if you did manage to go by there, then there would probably be a gargantuan line of women desperate to use the toilet. As a result of that for the last year or two of high school I had to pretty much wait until lunch time before I got a chance to go to the bathroom most of the times, and I spent most of the day frantically holding it and then running to the bathroom before lunch, and then most likely having to wait a good long while for the privilege.

Fortunately it wasn't as bad as it could have been. On the days when I had gym class, which was every other day pretty much, I could use the bathroom in the ladies locker room, so at least I got a second chance to go to the bathroom. And then the second year I only had a three or four hour day so I was able to get through the day with one bathroom break but I would still usually spend a portion of the day, pretty much every day for the last two years of high school, where I really really had to pee!

But that wasn't even the most frustrating part of the entire situation. No, the most frustrating part of that was of course, again my personal pet peeve, the fact is that all of the boys' bathrooms were still open! Since they only found drugs and alcohol in the girls bathroom they only locked the ladies rooms, but the boys' restrooms on all three floors were still completely open for business. Not only that, again another pet peeve of mine, is that the boys had far more places to pee in general. I asked some of my friends and they informed me that the boys' restroom had three stalls but they also had seven urinals. So that means that every boys bathroom had 10 places to pee and they had three of them in the building. So that meant that for the last two years of high school there was a situation where the boys had about 30 places to pee, resulting in about one toilet for every 25 boys, ensuring never a wait, while the entire female student body had to deal with making do with those measly five toilets in the girls bathroom down by the nurses office.

Needless to say my male friends all thought that this was screamingly hilarious. Since they knew that I would try to go to the bathroom between every class, because you never know if there is going to be a line, so you take every opportunity that you can to try and use the bathroom. If you go between classes and the line is out the door and you only have four minutes to get to class on time you are basically out of luck. So if I found a bathroom that was open and available I would make sure to take every chance to use it!

But for the remainder of those two years every day was sort of a crazy situation where I'd be walking to class with my friends and they would go into the boys bathroom and I would kick the door to the girls restroom, which was locked, and curse under my breath, and of course they found this to be hilarious. And then they knew the reason why I would take 20 minutes to get to lunch was because I was waiting in the one girls bathroom that was open to so I could freaking pee! These situations were all extremely frustrating, but I think it was around then I started to start realizing my fetish for female desperation, and even though I am a lesbian, one of the situations I seem to find most exciting is a situation where the boys are able to go to the bathroom and the girls are forced to go on holding it.

However I think that the real main inspiration for this novella came from chatting with people in online communities who share the interest in this fetish. I have chatted with many men and women alike who shared interest in female desperation, and the interesting thing is that most women into desperation have the fetish as a result of being desperate, whereas most men who have the fetish developed the fetish from seeing women desperate. This I think creates a bit of a divide between male and female fans of desperation. Female fans of female desperation have had to live the experience, whereas men just get a free show, having rarely experienced desperation themselves. I'm not saying that male desperation never happens or that there aren't situations where men are forced to hold it, but in most situations a guy can find some alternative even if a bathroom is not available or get to go without waiting. Women I think tend to be encouraged to hold it in most situations. A result of social conditioning's based on misogyny, maybe, but at any rate women are forced to stoically endure holding it while the men can just go wherever they want and that seems to be true pretty much everywhere in the world.

But the primary inspiration for this novella came from a guy I used to talk to about female desperation. While we both love seeing women desperate, and I have to admit it's fun to be desperate within limits, he couldn't seem to comprehend the idea that most women were not into being desperate when they really wanted to go to the bathroom. Even women who are into female desperation sometimes, if not usually, want to be able to just go to the bathroom when they are preoccupied with other things. You do not want to be walking around with a full bladder while you are trying to attend some type of activity or have to miss out on going to the bathroom because the lines too long or just have to endure incredible bladder pain in an inconvenient situation. Even those who find the experience sexually arousing might not want to have to experience that in a public situation, which actually just makes the whole situation even more awkward!

However when it came to female desperation all he could think about was how great it would be to see women disadvantaged when it came to relieving themselves. He said about how he would like a world without any form of potty parity and where he could open a nightclub where he could severely shortchange women on the number of bathrooms, not that it's not already done now seeing as most architects are men! But he also said he liked the idea of going around and putting out of order signs on the ladies rooms as a way of promoting desperation and just inconveniencing women who have to pee in general. The character of James is largely based on him.

Here is where I feel a similar conflict to the character in my novella, who again is totally based on me in pretty much every way. The fact is from a pure standpoint as a lover of desperation I can appreciate the genius behind that idea.

And as a person with a really good sense of humor in general I have to admit that that's a pretty hilarious prank, not going to lie, I would probably find that to be rather funny except for one minor detail that I sum up with my favorite dialogue from the entire novella that I think nicely sums up the entire point that I was trying to make throughout the entire narrative:

Jill couldn't help but burst out laughing. "Okay I'll be the first to admit it, it really is fucking hilarious, and even I cannot deny that. It's evil, but sometimes the evilest pranks are the funniest ones. Honestly the whole idea is somewhat ingenious and I have to applaud your brilliance in thinking of such a nefarious plan. But I do just have one teensy-weensy little problem with it."

James scratched his head. "What am I forgetting?"

Jill rolled her eyes. "You don't see a problem with this?"

James shook his head once again. "No, the whole plan actually seems pretty well thought out; I don't see any possible flaws with the plan."

Jill stood there tapping her foot. "Really, you don't see a single flaw with the plan? What was I just sort of lecturing you guys about not long ago? You don't see a problem here?"

Jack and James looked at each other shrugged their shoulders and shook their heads.

"Really you guys don't see a problem here perhaps from my perspective at the idea of you guys locking the women's restroom?" Jill suddenly started dancing around and put her hands up to her breasts and started jingling them around and then did a flip of her hair before spinning around. "I'm a woman numbskulls! If you lock all of the ladies rooms up as well as the men's room, then what am I supposed to do?! You totally were oblivious to the fact that while you were planning this whole lock the ladies room scheme up that the third co-conspirator in your group is a woman, a woman with a practical need to urinate at some point over the course of the entire day!"

James laughed. "Oh wow, I guess I forgot about that."

"Of course you did, you guys never seem to think about anything other than seeing women desperate!" Jill said as she pointed to herself. "I on the other hand have to consider the practical implications of all these evil little plans we think of. Granted I will admit that it's a hilarious idea, but you can see why it wouldn't work out well for me."

"It reminds me of something that I did once," James said laughing. "Once I went around putting all of these out of order signs on all these ladies rooms when they were perfectly available. It was funny because I saw these women going up to the bathroom and looking at the sign and frowning and the looks on their faces, absolutely priceless!"

"Oh my God that is so freaking wrong!" Jill shouted shaking her head.

"Although I will admit that it probably was priceless to see the looks on their faces. I am sure that the look on my face the few times I have seen an out of order sign on the toilet must have been a Kodak moment, but still you can see why I couldn't really go through with this whole plan. Not just because it seems especially malicious, even if it would be hilarious, but because practically speaking it would not end well for me."

I think that this pretty much sums up the entire novella and all of my attitudes towards the situation. If I was with a guy like him and he suggested something like that I would think it was funny but I ultimately would not go through with it. Because of purely practical and selfish concerns, I would not lock myself out of a bathroom for 4 to 6 hours when I know I'm going to need one! However if someone did that to me, while I know that I would definitely be furious, I couldn't be entirely angry because I would see the hilarity in it, and I honestly do have a very good sense of humor about these things, but believe me I would be furious and I would be absolutely fuming. The same thing is true about the whole situation in the beginning of going to a concert simply to witness lines to the restroom. It would be fun to watch, but I know that at some point I would also have to participate, whereas any guys who might be along for the free show get just that, a free show with no desperation for them whatsoever.

That pretty much sums up my thoughts on the matter, at least in brief, I could easily ramble on and on but I think that I have made my point. The last thing I would just like to mention is that I originally had a different ending to the story. Originally it was going to end with Jill going to a rest stop and just finding that the door there was locked in another bit of poetic justice and irony (some of my favorite situations involve revenge desperation and people becoming the victims of their own bad behavior) and then screaming as she realized that. But then I decided that after all that she had been through she deserved a more exciting ending involving nonmutual nudity, tickle torture and female dominant sex with an Asian woman, all lesbian fantasies of mine that I hope someday to fulfill. All in all I think that I made the right decision and I am sure that you will probably agree. I hope that this is a novella that both male and female fans of female desperation can appreciate on all different levels.

And just one final word, yes I am not lying when I say that I did write this entire novella while desperate. For a long time I had wanted to try writing a desperation story while bursting myself so that I could better relate to my desperate protagonist and I decided that I would try that with this novella. So each time I was getting ready to write I would drink a bunch, read and edit the previous chapters that I had written on previous nights, then I wouldn't allow myself to go to the bathroom until I had finished writing a couple of chapters at which point I was about ready to scream and explode. I did abandon this somewhat towards the later chapters though because after holding for hours on end while writing for several days in a row my bladder was getting really seriously sore and I found myself peeing more than usual and I thought that I had better cool it.

But I thought that it was an interesting gimmick to try and I have read somewhere that people supposedly make better decisions with a full bladder and work harder, which might be attributed to the fact that you want to get to a bathroom, so you focus very hard on the situation and completing the task at hand. After writing this novella with my legs crossed and my bladder bursting, I honestly think that there is something to that! I managed to write this entire thing in about five days which is the fastest I have ever written something of this length before, and I think I owe it to the fact that I wrote it while squirming in desperation and aching for a pee! At any rate I hope that it made the writing of this novella better and I hope you enjoy knowing that I suffered for my art!

I have many more ideas for desperation stories and novellas that I will surely publish at some point in the future but in the meantime you can check out some of my desperate experiences and stories, both true and fictional, in my blog at https://desperatejill.livejournal.com/. Also if you're interested you can take my long ladies room line poll at https://www.misterpoll.com/polls/540072.